THE RADIO MENACE

The Apes of Devil's Island

BY JOHN CUNNINGHAM

The Darkness at Windon Manor

BY MAX BRAND

The Exploits of Beau Quicksilver

BY FLORENCE M. PETTEE

The Flying Legion

BY GEORGE ALLAN ENGLAND

The Golden Cat:
The Adventures of Peter the Brazen, Volume 3

BY LORING BRENT

The Opposing Venus: The Complete Cabalistic Cases
of Semi Dual, the Occult Detector

BY J.U. GIESY AND JUNIUS B. SMITH

The Ruby of Suratan Singh: The Adventures
of Scarlet and Bradshaw, Volume 2

BY THEODORE ROSCOE

The Sheriff of Tonto Town:
The Complete Tales of Sheriff Henry, Volume 2

BY W.C. TUTTLE

The Vengeance of the Wah Fu Tong:
The Complete Cases of Jigger Masters, Volume 1

BY ANTHONY M. RUD

THE RADIO MENACE

RALPH MILNE FARLEY

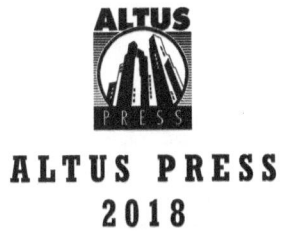

ALTUS PRESS
2018

TABLE OF CONTENTS

FOREWORD

THE MOST IMPORTANT news stories never get onto the front page. For a number of years I have been keeping a scrapbook of obscure newspaper clippings about events which, little noted at the time, were to make history.

The collection starts with half a "stick"—paragraph—of filler from a newspaper of June 29, 1914, telling how some unimportant nobleman and his wife were shot by a crazy student in some never-before-heard-of city in the Balkans. Sarajevo, I think the name was. You've probably heard of the war to which it led.

Then there is the Boston *Post* clipping of July 1, 1919, telling of the mysterious disappearance of Myles Standish Cabot from his Back Bay radio laboratory. He turned up later on the planet Venus, as you doubtless recall.

And the clipping about the escaped lunatic from the Danvers asylum, terrorizing an electric plant in Lynn. It wasn't a lunatic at all, but rather that same Myles Cabot, transmitting himself back to earth by wireless.

And the clipping about two game-hunting young aviators being lost on the Greenland ice-cap in the spring of 1926. They were really Eric Redmond and Angus Selkirk of the Milwaukee *Eagle* polar expedition, and they weren't lost. They eventually discovered the north polar orifice, the existence of which science now admits.

And the clipping about Scarface Boston Jimmy quitting the bootleg racket in the spring of 1929, and moving out. He followed Eric and Angus to the land of the Vikings inside the earth, and shot up things quite badly there before he got through.

And then—but wait until you hear this one!

The Boston *Post* of June 3, 1931, contained the following item under date-line of Rockingham Junction, N.H.:

> The B. & M. agent here reports seeing a large dragon as big as a horse, with leathery batlike wings, fly over the station at about five o'clock this morning. The agent had been to a lodge party the night before. It is reported that it was some party.

I saved this clipping for two reasons. First, because I used to cover Rockingham County myself for the *Post*, and used to receive twenty-five cents apiece for inventing fillers like that. Secondly, because I am interested in pterodactyls and other prehistoric beasts.

But it was not until some time later that I added this clipping to my collection of obscure items about events which were afterward discovered to be epoch-making.

Nor does the world yet realize that that news-story is entitled to take its place with the assassination at Sarajevo. It is time that the world knew. Hence this account which I am now writing.

The flame which was kindled at Sarajevo required tens of millions of men to stamp it out.

Two men and a girl, with some assistance from a few friends, confronted the menace represented by that Rockingham Junction winged monster, which threatened the free existence of the whole human race. For a greater Kaiser than Wilhelm set out to dominate the world in 1931.

I NOTED only the one item at the time; and did not realize how many people throughout the United States thought they were seeing things until the *Literary Digest* compiled a collection of accounts of over four hundred separate similar apparitions. Congressmen Tinkham of Massachusetts and Schafer of

Wisconsin promptly made this the text for a renewed demand for the repeal of the Volstead Act. Public interest was at last aroused. Seeing the dragon, usually in the early morning or at twilight, became the most popular outdoor sport.

The mythical beast was even reported to have been seen on the same evening at such widely separated points as Boston and San Francisco. This at first was scoffed at, until a leading professor of aerodynamics wrote a Sunday syndicate article, in which he proved, to his own satisfaction at least, that with the wing-spread claimed for the creature, it could easily have flown across the continent in the period represented between Eastern Standard Time and Pacific Standard Time.

Finally a certain circus king claimed to have killed the beast, and made considerable money by exhibiting its stuffed carcass at a dollar a head, children twenty-five cents. At this, every one came to believe that the whole matter had been a colossal hoax, for the mere purpose of laying the foundation for this very exhibit; that the showman had planted a few news-stories, and the contagion of mass imagination had supplied the rest. Popular interest suddenly lagged, and a new sensation took its place—for the public must at all times have its pet sensation. This was the remarkable increase in missing persons.

Then the missing persons were in turn forgotten—by all except their loved ones—and the front pages were given over to the next new sensation, whatever that may have been. I have forgotten.

CHAPTER I

LARRY GETS A CLUE

THE UNEXPLAINED DISAPPEARANCE of Assistant United States Attorney Eliot Endicott from his office in the Federal Building, Boston, ought to have attracted more notice than it did. All that appeared in the press was a brief notice that young Endicott had left his bachelor apartment in the evening, had told the night clerk that he was bound for his office, and had not been seen since. It came just too late to be featured as a part of the missing persons epidemic.

The Department of Justice did not give out the fact that Endicott had actually reached his office, accompanied by Operative Riley, his personal bodyguard; had bolted the door on the inside, leaving Riley on guard in the hall; had been heard to call for help; and had totally disappeared while rescuers were battering down the door.

One reason why these facts were withheld was that they sounded preposterous, and the Department feared ridicule. Another and more vital reason was that the missing man had been engaged in a highly confidential investigation of the establishment and gradual development of a gang of super-intelligent criminals in Boston, and accordingly the Department did not wish this gang to realize what a haul they had made, or that the Department had any clues whatever as to what had become of the young assistant.

The Department did not wish the gang to know how many

clues it had, and was equally unwilling to have the public know how few; for the clues were indeed nearly negligible.

On the evening of Eliot Endicott's disappearance, Lawrence Larrabee, a young reporter of the Boston *Post,* happened to be on his way from the newspaper office on Washington Street to the South Station, bound home for the night. It was dark and sultry. Heat lightning was playing in the distance. The streets were practically deserted.

"A fine night for a murder," thought Larry, "in which case I hope I get the scoop."

As he passed through Post Office Square, he thought he heard a leathery flapping overhead. Involuntarily, he looked up. The lightning flickered, and he thought he saw outlined the huge shape of a pterodactyl winging through the night.

"Too bad the flying dragon is no longer news," he said to himself. "This would have made a good story a few months ago. I wonder if the beast was stealing any mail. Guess I'll go into the Federal Building and find out if any one else saw him. Perhaps I can make up a story out of it after all."

So he turned and mounted the steps. He had followed pure hunches before, and they had led to news.

Downstairs the building was deserted, but he heard an air-hammer at work on the second floor. Following the sound, he found Operative Riley, several policemen, the night watchman, and the wrecking crew engaged in breaking into Eliot Endicott's office. The door-frame crashed inward just as he arrived. The rescuers rushed in, and Larry followed them. But the room was empty.

"Gone!" exclaimed "Mr. Endicott is gone! He was here a minute ago. He hollered for help. We broke down the door, and now he's gone!"

The office seemed normal except for the absence of the assistant district attorney.

Here was a story, a whale of a story! Young Larrabee got all the details from Riley, then hastened back to the city room of the *Post*. He hunted through the filed clippings which news-paper men call the "morgue" to write up a full biography of the victim. But he carefully omitted all mention of the flying dragon; he would save that for later. Turning his story in to the night editor, he sped back to the Federal Building.

Nothing further had developed. Riley and a squad of police and Secret Service operatives were on guard. So Larry chummed around with them, smoked innumerable cigarettes, and waited.

ALONG toward morning, newsboys began crying their papers in the streets below. Larry bought one of each variety. The *Herald* and the *Globe* had merely a brief paragraph, announcing Eliot Endicott's disappearance. Then the *Post* appeared.

Larrabee's story was not on the front page. That was strange! Feverishly he thumbed the sheets looking for it, and at last found—not his story, but rather merely the same brief item as had come out in the *Herald* and the *Globe*.

Suppressed! That was what had happened. His great scoop had been suppressed. For a moment he was horribly disap-pointed, and then he was glad.

He made up his mind to follow out his hunch about the pterodactyl. His paper was the only one to have any information, any clues so far. The scoop would be all the greater, if and when he succeeded in locating the missing assistant district attorney.

Shortly after sunrise the district attorney arrived, visibly agitated. So agitated, in fact, that he didn't notice Larry's pres-ence.

Striding into the room, the official glanced quickly around. Then he asked Riley for a full report, taking notes as Riley explained. Larry also scribbled on the back of an envelope what few points had been omitted before.

When the interrogation had been completed, the district attorney put his hand under the edge of the desk of his missing assistant, and pushed something. Then he walked over to one of the bookcases which lined the walls of the room and tugged

The bird flew at them with uncanny persistence.

at it. It swung forward, showing a cavity behind; in this cavity were the steel doors of a large wall safe.

It was now broad daylight. The inevitable pigeons which infest the ledges of every down town building in Boston were parading up and down, preening themselves in the morning sunshine, and chattering: "Look—look—look—at a coo! Look—look—look—at a coo!" to each other. Morning had come.

"Those infernal birds will drive me crazy," muttered the district attorney, as he twirled the knobs of the safe.

So Riley went to the window and shooed them away. They circled with much flapping and returned.

The doors of the safe opened at last, and the district attorney pounced on a small red leatherboard packet bound with tape.

"It's here!" he exclaimed. "They didn't get it, after all!"

Extricating the package, he flung it down on the desk.

"Watch that!" he admonished the operative. "I'll see if there's anything missing."

As he returned to the safe and knelt before it, one of the pigeons flew in the window, and straight at Riley's face. Riley beat it away, but it came at him again and again, pecking at his eyes, driving him back into a corner. The policeman and other operatives rushed to the poor Irishman's assistance. The packet on the desk lay unguarded. The district attorney rose to his feet, and turned to see what was the matter.

At that instant another pigeon swooped in through the window, seized the packet in its beak, and swooped out again. The district attorney rushed to the window and hurled a law book after the departing bird which promptly dropped its precious burden and soared away.

Larry followed the official to the window. They both leaned far out. A short thick-set man, with a cap pulled low over his face, was pacing up and down on the sidewalk below. As the red packet thumped upon the concrete, this man snatched it up, and jumped into an auto which was standing beside the curb, with its engine running. The car promptly sped off with its prize.

"After them!" shouted the district attorney. "They've got Mr. Endicott's secret report."

The bird which had been attacking Riley now soared out and joined its mate.

Every one rushed to the street. But it was too late. Not a sign of the departing car. Police headquarters were promptly notified by phone, but no one was able to give an adequate description of either the thieves or their auto.

WHEN all the excitement had finally quieted down, the district attorney noticed Larrabee.

"Who are you?" he bellowed.

"Reporter for the Boston *Post*, sir," Larry explained, exhibiting his badge.

"What the devil are you doing here?"

"Getting the story, of course."

"Hey, one of you cops, take this bird into custody. He may be mixed up in this."

So, despite Larry's protests, he was manacled and marched

off to the police station. An hour or so later, however, he was released, and ordered to report at once to his boss.

The editor received the reporter in his sanctum, and carefully closed the door.

"Well, Larry," said he, "you got a good scoop. I've read it. I'm sorry that the night editor had to kill it; but we've promised to cooperate with the department, as you've probably guessed. Now I understand from the district attorney that you've gone and got a lot more information that you ought not to have. Good boy! Of course, have to kill that, too, but they can't keep it suppressed forever. Now, tell me the whole story."

So Larrabee told him everything, not omitting even the pterodactyl nor the two pigeons.

When he had finished, the editor remarked, "It sounds perfectly crazy. No wonder the authorities are leery about its appearing in print. I take it that you have a hunch that the winged dragon flew off with young Endicott?"

"I can't believe it—but I think that's it."

"Well, none of the other papers appear to be in on the story at all. Have you any plans for running down your clues?"

"Yes, sir."

"All right. Go and get it. I've followed your hunches before. Sometimes they're positively uncanny. Go up to the city room, take your typewriter, and write out all that you know, and what you plan to do. Seal it up and bring it to me. Then go and get that story! I hope you scoop the authorities as well as the other papers."

"Yes, sir."

Later in the morning, Lawrence Larrabee handed his chief a sealed envelope.

"Where now?" asked the editor.

"I'd rather not say it aloud," replied the reporter. "There's a pigeon on your window ledge, and he might overhear me."

The editor guffawed.

"This thing seems to be getting on your nerves," said he. Then, sobering, "And yet I don't know but what you are right. Follow your hunch to the end, Larry. Go and get it."

The pigeon cocked its head on one side, just as if it were listening, and then soared off down Washington Street.

Larrabee hastened to the North Station, where he purchased a ticket to Rockingham Junction, N.H. He was going there first, because he had ascertained from the files of his newspaper that that was where the winged monster had made its initial appearance that spring.

A man stood behind him in the waiting line at the ticket window. This man also bought a ticket to Rockingham Junction and followed Larry onto the train.

Later that morning both of them got off at the junction. It had been Larry's plan to interview the station agent, who was reported to have been the first to see the pterodactyl, but the other man beat him to the window.

Larry hung around until the other had transacted his business. Then he in turn approached the window, while the other retired to one of the waiting room seats and furtively watched him.

The station agent was seated at the telegraph instruments, so the young reporter leaned against the counter waiting, and idly turning over in his mind how to broach the matter to the agent, who quite likely had been kidded about the dragon until he was very touchy on the subject.

As Larry waited, he suddenly heard his own name—slightly misspelled, it is true—ticked off by the agent. Telegraphy happened to be one of his accomplishments; used to cover sporting events. Instantly he was all alert.

The agent finished sending, and closed the switch. Back came the repeat from the other end: "Washington Jones, Intervale, N.H. Reporter named Laraby here on King's trail, Send reënforcements quick. Jackson."

"Aha!" said the newspaper man to himself. "So I'm shadowed, am I? Well, I guess that means I'm hot on the trail!"

Then to the station agent, as the latter approached the window, " A time-table, please."

LARRY perused the time-table. Then, his plans made up, he went outside and hailed a taxi. The man who had been following him promptly got into a green taxi next in line.

"About three miles out the Exeter road," announced the reporter in a loud voice, then leaning forward he spoke quietly in the driver's ear: "I'm being shadowed. Can you shake that other car?"

"Can I, eh?" replied the taxi man. "You're on, buddy. Just watch me."

In a few moments they drew up in front of his company's garage. The green cab drew up just behind them.

Larry's driver turned around and shouted at him through the glass partition, "Sorry, sir, but the ignition's loose again. And we haven't another car. Would you mind waiting until I fix it? It'll only take a minute or two."

"All right. All right," Larry shouted back, with mock testiness. "Only please hurry."

So the driver honked, the garage doors swung open, and they drove in.

"Quick, buddy, this way," commanded the taxi man. "I've another car in the alley back of the garage."

And soon they were hurrying to the station again, while the man who had been following him sat patiently in the green taxi outside the garage, watching through a window the top of the taxi inside, to make sure they didn't leave. And with his meter running!

Larry rewarded his friend with a five-dollar bill, and bought a ticket to Boston, inquiring ostentatiously about the time of departure and arrival of the train, its accommodations, and so forth. Then he went out onto the platform.

The train for Boston arrived and left. The northbound limited stopped for water and went on again. A worried-looking man dashed into the station and up to the window.

"Say," he blurted out, "was there a young fellow in a dark blue suit here just now?"

"I'll say there was!" replied the agent. "He talked me deaf, dumb and blind about the accommodations to Boston."

"Where is he now?" asked the other eagerly.

"On his way to Boston, I guess," replied the agent. "He bought a ticket for there, and got onto the train. There is another in twenty minutes, to save you from asking."

"Then take this wire," said the man, and he hurriedly wrote out, "Washington Jones, Intervale, N.H. Never mind Laraby. He give me the slip back to Boston. Jackson."

"That's two words extra," remarked the agent with New England thrift.

"Hell!" replied the man. " What do I care!"

Meanwhile Lawrence Larrabee was settling himself comfortably in the northbound limited, *en route* for Intervale, New Hampshire. There must be something to his hunch, after all, for how could that man have happened to follow him, unless the pigeon outside the window of the editor of the *Post* had actually overheard, and had told on him? Of course, he had taken great care not to say where he was going; but if the pigeon had even overheard him say that he was on the trail of Eliot Endicott, that might account for this man following him. And if pigeons could act human—a fantastic theory that was strongly borne out by the actions of the two that had stolen the packet from the Federal Building—then might not the pterodactyl be human too, and in cahoots with whoever had made away with Eliot Endicott?

At this point he was diverted from his thoughts by noticing the girl across the aisle. A pippin! Larry promptly forgot all about his quest. Here was the neatest thing in skirts that he had ever seen. Promptly he resolved to make this young lady's acquaintance at the earliest possible moment. He noticed particularly that there was no ring on the important finger.

But his hopes were dashed by the arrival, from another car, of a stern and forbidding male parent. A distinguished-looking gentleman at that, gray-haired, black-mustached and courtly.

Larry was no mean detective. His career on the Boston *Post*, including his work on the present case, had demonstrated that. Now he planned to devote his talents to discovering the identity of the beautiful girl.

He listened intently to her conversation with her father, in the hope of hearing some clue, but all that he learned was that the girl's name appeared to be "Helen." There was a "K" on one of their bags, and another bag bore a tag, which, however, was turned blank side up.

When father and daughter went to the diner, Larry pounced on this tag, and turned it over; but it was blank on the other side, too. Then he followed them into the diner, but was unable to get a seat near them.

When they all returned to the parlor car, he heard them mention "Bartlett." Was that a station or a man's name? He felt a twinge of jealousy, until he had looked it up in his time-table and found that it was the name of a station just beyond Intervale.

At Portland they all changed trains. The girl and her father took the same train that Larry did, namely the Maine Central for Intervale and Bartlett.

WHEN the train stopped at Intervale, Larry's destination, he stayed on, and got off with the pair at Bartlett. The criminals and their pet pterodactyl could wait; he had more important business on hand just now. At that, it might after all be well for him to leave the train at some other station than Intervale, and so divert suspicion from himself. Thus he kidded himself into believing that his duty coincided with his pleasure.

It was quite late in the evening when the train reached Bartlett, and somehow he lost the girl and her father in the crowd at the station, nor did any one of whom he inquired seem to recognize the pair from his description of them.

So he put up at a hotel for the night, registering as "John O'Brien," as his real name and the fact that he was on the trail of the missing attorney were known to the latter's abductors.

All the next day he spent wandering around the town in the hope of catching a glimpse of his fair quarry. It was not until late in the afternoon that his patience was rewarded, for he saw her enter the post office.

As he followed her in he heard the postmaster say to her, "Here's a letter for you. It was addressed to the lumber camp, but I guess it's for you, all right."

The girl tore it open, threw the envelope in the wastebasket, and started to read the letter. Then gasped and staggered backward, clutching a desk for support. It looked as though she were going to faint.

Larry's first impulse was to spring to her assistance. But his agile mind quickly realized that, unless she actually fainted, such an action on his part would be likely to bar forever any chance which he might have of acquaintance with the young lady. So while she gasped and clung to the edge of the desk with the hand which held the letter, he stepped forward as though hunting for a pen, and read rapidly the contents of the letter thus displayed before him.

What he read caused him to gasp, too. But with an effort he steadied himself. The girl by this time had recovered her composure. She carefully reread the letter; then folded it, stuffed it in one of her pockets, and hurried out of the building.

Larry retrieved her envelope from the wastebasket, glanced at it quickly, thrust it into his pocket and approached the delivery window.

"That was Miss Helyn Kent, wasn't it?" he asked.

"Yes," answered the postmaster guardedly.

"I thought I recognized her," Larry continued. "An old friend of mine. Haven't seen her for several years. But she didn't seem to recognize me. What's she doing up here?"

"Staying at the Mortons'," was the reply. "You know the Morton camp? Well, she and her dad take the camp for a few weeks 'most every summer, while the Mortons themselves are away."

"Then it's me for the Mortons'!" announced Larry jubilantly.

CHAPTER II

THE GIANT BEAST

MEANWHILE THE MISSING assistant district attorney, whom Larry had set out to find, was becoming the storm center of this gigantic world-menace which is about to be related.

Eliot Endicott was only recently out of Harvard Law School, where he had stood nearly at the head of his class. While in the school he had been one of the most active organizers of the Intercollegiate Republican League, in recognition of which activity he had landed the assistant district attorney-ship almost immediately upon graduation. As he was possessed of a keen, inquiring and analytical mind, the district attorney finally assigned to him the investigation of the clever criminal band whose activities were worrying New England.

The records of the investigation he kept in his office, which was amply reënforced against robbery.

The windows had burglar-proof catches, and were also wired to a burglar-alarm system, so contrived that if any window were opened, except during regular office-hours, a gong would ring in the corridor of the building, and a light would flash both in the office of the burglar-alarm company and also at city police headquarters.

To cut the wires of the system, for the purpose of preventing the sounding of the alarm, would have exactly the opposite effect, and would sound it at once, for it was a break circuit rather than a make circuit. To render assurance doubly sure, in case the apparatus should get out of order, all messages were also transmitted, both to police headquarters and to the burglar-patrol company, from a radio set within the room.

Inside the windows there were heavy steel shutters with Yale locks.

The door was reënforced with steel, and hitched up to the same system as the windows, but with one exception, namely, that although the window-alarm could be switched off from within the room, the door-alarm could only be switched off at company headquarters after a visit from an inspector. This requirement of a visit from an inspector was an additional precaution, to make sure that whoever opened the door was an authorized person.

Even when the burglar-alarm company was notified that Endicott himself was on the way to his office, they nevertheless sent over the inspector, lest some one else might reach the office first and impersonate Endicott.

In addition to this system, Endicott was personally guarded with the utmost care. Everywhere he went he was accompanied by an operative of the Department of Justice and was shadowed by still other operatives.

On the evening in question he entered the Federal Building in the company of Operative Riley and an inspector from the burglar-alarm company whom he had brought along for the speedy turning off of the alarm. On the way up to his office on the second floor he spoke to the night watchman and to the foreman of the night wrecking-crew, which were engaged in the remodeling of part of the building.

Of course, when he unlocked and opened his door, the gong in the corridor set up a tremendous clatter which reverberated ominously through the empty building, and did not cease when he entered and closed the door from the inside. The inspector then hurried back to his company to turn off the gong, and Riley placed himself on guard just outside the door.

Endicott bolted the door on the inside. He then switched on the lights, switched off the window burglar-alarm, unlocked the steel shutters, and unlatched the windows, opening them wide to let some air into the stuffy office, for the season was summer. While he was doing this, the clatter of the gong outside his door ceased, thus indicating that the inspector had returned to the company. The young attorney heard a policeman arrive, receive Riley's report that everything was O.K., and depart.

AS ENDICOTT flung open the last window, a man who had been crouching on the sill outside leaped in upon him. The intruder had the advantage of being thoroughly prepared and rehearsed. Endicott being taken by surprise, was forced backward by the onslaught; and before he could recover his balance, the intruder had seized Endicott's coat by the lapels, and had pulled it down off his shoulders, pinioning his upper arms.

At first the young attorney was too startled to call for help. Then, as he collected his senses, he realized that calling for help would do no good, for the office door was bolted on the inside. So he might just as well devote his attentions to his assailant, and leave the faithful Riley out of consideration for the present.

For a moment the two men stared into each other's faces. Endicott studied his captor. The man was thick-set, almost apelike in his proportions, with long gangling arms, red hair, and a pugilistic face dotted with freckles. His features, especially his eyes, were indescribably non-human.

Eliot Endicott, although rather slightly built, was hard as nails, and had in fact at one time held the college championship in catch-as-catch-can wrestling. He knew that when one's arms are pinioned by one's coat in the manner in which the red-headed intruder now held him, there is only a single possible way to get free, and that the chances are very strongly against even that way succeeding unless the enemy is taken completely by surprise. That way consists in violently throwing one's hands in a circle: outward, upward, inward and downward. This gets one's coat back on, and one's assailant's hands off, at the same time. So he kicked the red-headed ape-man suddenly in the shins to divert his attention, and then rapidly executed the above-described movement.

The movement wrenched the man's hands from Endicott's lapels, Endicott's coat slid properly back onto his shoulders once more, and his fists drove square at the face of the redhead.

Evidently the red-head was not the pugilist which he looked, for he neither ducked nor warded off the blow. Instead he took it on the point of the jaw, and dropped to the floor without a sound.

"One-two-three-four-five-six-seven-eight-nine-ten," counted the official, grinning broadly, in spite of the rather mashed condition of his knuckles. "Oh, Riley!"

"Yes, sir," came the operative's voice from outside the door. "What's the trouble?"

"No trouble at all, Riley. Merely that I've caught a robber in my office. Just a minute, while I unbolt the door, and you can come in and help me truss him up."

But as Endicott walked toward the door, a voice behind him said in a low but peremptory tone, " Halt! Halt, or I fire!"

Endicott had served in the National Guard. He knew a military command when he heard one. He halted.

"Now stick 'em up!"

Promptly he raised his hands aloft.

"I'm sorry," continued the voice, "but you'll have to stand just like that until Red comes out of his trance, unless the King takes it into his head to go back and bring another man, which isn't likely. Your *second* serious mistake, Eliot, was in not remembering that rattlesnakes hunt in pairs. You may recall that the snake-man of the New York zoo, after a lifetime of experience, died a couple of years ago in the New jersey mountains, due to that same error."

"And my *first* mistake?" asked Endicott coolly, still holding his hands aloft. "What was that?"

"That," laughed the voice, "was in bolting your office door on the inside."

As if to emphasize the point, Riley began pounding on the outside of the door, and calling, "Are you all right, sir?"

"Better tell him yes," admonished the voice quietly.

"Yes, Riley," replied Endicott hurriedly. "The robber is still out cold, and I'll get to the door in a moment, unless he receives reënforcements."

"Careful," cautioned the voice.

Red groaned and blinked his eyes.

"Red," commanded the voice, "snap out of it! What did he do to you?"

"Dunno," said Red stupidly, feeling of his jaw.

"I slugged him, right on the button," explained Endicott, rather proudly.

With a snarl, Red sprang to his feet and rushed him. As they grappled, Endicott got a glimpse at the other intruder, the owner of the voice. He was a young man of just about Endicott's age. His build was slightly heavier, but not so athletic. His face was Semitic, rather attractive, and certainly strong and intellectual. In his hand was an automatic. He had the pleasing personality of the typical English Jew. And his captive almost liked him in spite of the situation. There was something strangely familiar about him, too.

Even as Endicott took all this in, he realized that the gun-wielder didn't dare to fire for fear of hitting Red; so the attorney started shouting to his faithful Riley for help.

"Cut that out, or I'll drill both of you," commanded the voice. "Let go of him, Red, or you'll stop a ton of lead."

The two broke and separated.

Riley pounded on the door outside. Then, "Hold out! I'll have help in a minute!" and the pounding ceased.

"**YOU SEE,** as I have already told you, you shouldn't have bolted the door," deprecated the man with the automatic. Then, turning to his henchman, "Red, I'm ashamed of you. Why be so vengeful? You may have a new-soul, and I may not, but you sometimes act in the most unsoulful manner. Here, truss this fellow up."

Going to the window, he produced from the ledge a coil of rope which he tossed to Red, who clumsily but effectively bound their angry captive and placed him in a chair.

"And now," inquired the other, seating himself on the desk and pocketing the gun, "Where are those papers?"

"What papers?" temporized Endicott.

"Cigarette papers!" replied the other scornfully. "Don't be silly. Come, be quick about it. You know as well as I do what I'm here for. I want the manuscript of that epochal crime-report which you are writing."

"Oh, that!" Endicott continued to temporize.

"That isn't here."

"Where is it then?" snapped the other. "Quick. We haven't much time."

"I'd rather not tell," said Endicott, smiling in spite of his bonds, which Red had spitefully tied unnecessarily tight.

"There are ways of making you tell," announced his captor menacingly. But just then there came the sound of an air-hammer on the outside of the door-casing. Riley had returned with some of the workmen.

"Hell!" ejaculated the man with the gun, jumping down off the desk. Deftly he slipped a gag between Endicott's teeth, and a handkerchief across his eyes, and commanded, "To the window with him, Red. The King is still there."

So the captive was rushed to the window, and was slid out onto the ledge, wondering what means of escape they could use. But his thoughts were cut short by a pair of grappling hooks snatching him around the waist and swinging him off into space. With a slightly jerky motion, he was carried through the air for five or ten minutes, and then was deposited on what was evidently another window ledge, where hands seized him and slid him into a room.

For nearly half an hour he lay neglected on the floor. At last he heard the voice of his abductor and the closing of shutters. Then he was lifted to a chair and his gag and bandage were removed.

He was in a small office. His captor was smiling down at him in a friendly and ingratiating manner. Red and several other men, equally rough types and all equally unhuman, were in the room.

And a creature! Endicott gasped and recoiled as his gaze fell on the creature.

It was indescribable. A slate-colored bat-winged lizard, squatting on the floor with its head towering above the standing men. And that head. A narrow pointed beak four feet long, balanced by a kingfisher crest of about the same length, the whole being mounted on a long wrinkled neck, bent like that of a heron. Eyes, lidless and unblinking. The folded leathery wings protruded backward from its forepaws across its shoulders, like two swords carried on parade. Their spread would be nearly thirty feet when open.

"So it's true?" gasped the captive.

"What's true?" replied his abductor.

"All these newspaper yarns about the pterodactyl."

"They're mainly true all right, but unfortunate. The King at first was a bit incautious in showing himself and once the story was given a good start, it didn't matter whether he showed himself or not, the people kept right on imagining that they saw him. Fortunately, however, that Philadelphia showman played right into our hands by concocting a fake pterodactyl for exhibition purposes; and now everybody believes that there never was a real one, which is lucky for us. I'll venture to bet that, with all your cleverness, your investigations never suggested to you that the pterodactyl had any connection with this 'gang of master minds' of ours—to use the popular expression. How little people guess!"

"Has he any connection?" countered Endicott, eagerly.

"We shall let you judge of that when you become one of us,"

was the surprising answer. "And now," continued his captor, "I shall introduce myself. Don't you remember your undergraduate classmate, Aaron Cohen?"

"I thought you looked familiar," exclaimed Endicott. "May I ask you why I am your prisoner?"

"Not our prisoner," deprecated Cohen, "but rather our honored guest. You have been elected to membership in our organization, and this is your initiation."

"And if I decline the honor?"

"You won't," laughed Cohen. "No one ever does. Dr. Chapin attends to that. And now I am going to have you untied. I want you to make yourself at home here, while I get the laboratory ready for you. There are magazines on the table. It may take me as much as an hour."

"**YOUR** mention of a 'laboratory' sounds ominous," said Endicott. "Would you mind telling me what sort of an experiment you are planning to try on me?"

"No experiment at all," replied Cohen. "We're merely going to transmit you by wireless to the headquarters of our organization."

"You're kidding me, aren't you?"

Cohen studied him intently for a moment, and finally said, a bit triumphantly, "Well, you're supposed to be intelligent, you graduated at the head of our class at Harvard, you were prominent in Law School, you pose as an amateur detective, and you've been making an intensive study of our organization. Yet you haven't the slightest inkling of how far we have progressed scientifically ahead of the rest of the world. Does that answer your question?"

"I'll have to be shown," replied Endicott guardedly.

"Perhaps you wonder," continued his classmate, "just why I gave up my attempt to get you to tell where your report is hidden. That may come later, but for the present we have decided to send a couple of pigeons to watch what is done when your rescuers break into your office."

"Stool pigeons, you mean?" interrupted Endicott.

"No, just ordinary pigeons," continued Cohen, "the kind one feeds with peanuts on Boston Common. Only these particular pigeons are members of our organization. They have new-souls just like the King here, and the rest of us. You see, I am being very frank with you, for you are soon to become one of us. Now make yourself at home, while I go to the laboratory. Boris and Frank, you two watch Mr. Endicott. Don't bother him, unless he makes a noise, opens a window, tries to leave the room, or attacks either of you; in any of which cases shoot him and shoot to kill."

So saying, he and the pterodactyl and all but two of the men left the room.

The prisoner picked up a magazine, and turned its pages aimlessly for a few moments, his mind dulled by his predicament. The two gunmen watched him with expressionless animal faces.

Then Eliot Endicott suddenly had an idea. He searched through his pockets, and found a stamped envelope and some blank paper. As the two guards did not appear to be paying any particular attention to what he was doing, he hurriedly addressed the envelope to his girl cousin, Miss Helyn Kent, Charlesgate Apartments, Cambridge, Massachusetts. He picked her out because she was clever and discreet; furthermore a letter addressed to a girl was likely to attract less attention than one addressed to the authorities. On one of the sheets of paper he wrote:

DEAR HELYN:

The criminals whom I have been trailing have got me at last. The pterodactyl, which the newspapers were so full of this spring, is real; and he is one of the gang. He flew with me from my office window to some other office building, where they are now planning to send me by radio, from a laboratory elsewhere in this building to their headquarters, wherever that may be. This all sounds perfectly crazy, but don't waste any sympathy on my mental condition; save it for what these superminds may do to me.

The leader of the outfit appears to be Aaron Cohen, an old classmate of mine. Also he has mentioned a Dr. Chapin as being one of them. This is all that I know.

If I succeed in mailing this letter, the substation postmark may give some clue as to what part of the city this building is in. I judge that the building has wireless masts because of Cohen's mention of radio. I can see through the frosted glass door panels that this is room 715. There is no name on the door.

Get this letter to the district attorney.

In haste and with love,

Eliot.

He folded up the paper, put it in the envelope and slipped the latter into one of his pockets. So far, so good. Now to find some opportunity for mailing it. If worse came to worst, he could just drop it somewhere, and trust that the finder would deposit it in a mailbox.

Those stupid gunmen! With dull animal eyes, they had watched him write the letter, and had not interfered, nor even investigated what he was doing. They had received detailed instructions from Cohen just what to prevent the prisoner from doing, and as writing was not among the things prohibited, they had let him write. They seemed doped or hypnotized, curiously unhuman.

Very much pleased with himself, he picked up a magazine and tried to read. He felt instinctively that he ought to be nonchalant. Now that he had done all that could be done for the present, he ought calmly to become absorbed in a story. That was the way the hero would do in a Sax Rohmer Oriental mystery movie, and Eliot Endicott had considerable of the theatrical in his make-up.

But his mind refused to concentrate on the printed page in front of him. He cursed himself for his carelessness in letting himself get trapped; he wondered whether these clever outlaws would be able to find the manuscript of his voluminous report in his office; he speculated on the presence of his classmate Aaron Cohen as a prominent member of this band of criminals, and on the human intelligence of the huge pterodactyl and of "the pigeons with souls"whom Cohen had mentioned; he wondered if it were really possible to transmit persons through space, or whether this was but a euphemism for some other diabolical performance, electrocution for instance. And Helyn! Would she get his letter? Would she miss him and worry about him?

HE WAS absorbed in these thoughts when Aaron Cohen reëntered the room and announced, "All is ready. Follow me. Boris and Frank will follow you, and will shoot if you try to pull anything."

So saying, he led the way into the corridor of the office building. Eliot Endicott kept his eyes alert for clues, such as names on doors, or posted notices, giving the name of the building or its owners. But the building appeared to be a new one; every door was unlabeled. The assistant district attorney did not recognize the corridor as one that he had ever seen before in his life.

As they passed the elevators, he edged over near the mail-chute, with the precious letter palmed in his right hand.

But Cohen turned and saw him, as he raised that hand toward the chute.

"None of that!"snapped his young captor, then laughed and added, "Oh, go ahead and ring the button, if it amuses you. The elevators aren't running this time of night, so no one will answer you."

He grinned tauntingly, turned away again, and continued on his way down the hall.

Quick as a flash, Eliot Endicott slipped the letter into the chute.

Boris and Frank offered no objection. Had they not heard their boss tell the prisoner to go ahead with what he was doing?

This was the letter which Lawrence Larrabee read over Helyn

Kent's shoulder in the Bartlett Post Office, although neither of them knew then how the missive happened to reach Bartlett so promptly, inasmuch as its original address in Endicott's hand was Cambridge, Massachusetts.

CHAPTER III

SUPERSCIENTIFIC POWERS

JUST BEYOND THE elevators, they entered a room labeled: "708. Radio Laboratories." Too bad he couldn't have got that information into his letter to Helyn, but it was now too late. Nevertheless, the searchers would be looking for such a laboratory in the vicinity of an unlabeled room numbered 715. Every little bit would help.

So Eliot Endicott was feeling quite hopeful as he entered the laboratory behind Aaron Cohen, and followed by the two gunmen, Boris and Frank. Inside he found the pterodactyl, the rest of the gunmen, and one new person, bearded, bespectacled and sinister, dressed in a buff-colored smock.

Cohen introduced him as, "Dr. Wladimir Polakowski, my laboratory assistant."

The room was crowded with electrical equipment, including a motor-generator set, some large Tesla coils, a Cooper-Hewitt mercury interrupter, and a complicated switch-panel. In one corner was a curtained cubicle, about six feet each way.

Dr. Polakowski stepped briskly over to the cubicle, and pulled back the front curtain, disclosing an interior absolutely barren, except for three metal rods which met at one of the upper rear corners, from which point they projected at right angles to each other, one straight down to the floor, and the other two in two horizontal directions. They were of some unfamiliar metal which looked like a very pale brass with a slight iridescent greenish tinge.

"The coördinate axes of our matter-transmitting set," explained Cohen, "I'll show you how it works."

He clicked several times to the dragon, who lumbered into the cubicle, and squatted there as compactly as possible. Cohen and Dr. Polakowski walked carefully around the beast tucking in protruding portions of its anatomy, especially its wing-tips, in order to make sure that nothing projected beyond the coordinate axes.

"We have to be very careful," explained Cohen. "It would be tragic if any part of him got left behind."

Then he stepped over to the panel, adjusted a telephone headset to his head, and grasped two of the switches. Dr. Polakowski took one last careful look at the pterodactyl, then pulled the curtain closed.

"O.K., chief," he announced.

"Stand by to receive," spoke Cohen into the transmitter.

"All ready," came faintly from his earphones.

So he threw the two switches. There came a blinding flash and a strong smell of ozone.

"One, two, three, four," counted Cohen, with his eye on a watch, then restored the switches to neutral, "All right, doctor. All over."

Polakowski opened the curtains. The cubicle was empty.

But Eliot Endicott refused to be impressed.

"Old stuff!" he snorted. "I've seen that done on the stage."

Aaron Cohen sighed. He was determined to impress his erstwhile classmate. "Well, I'll even take a chance on one of these hunkies with the curtain open. Come on, Red."

The gunman thus addressed shrugged his shoulders, and picking up a steel chair, entered the cubicle with it, and sat down.

"Watch closely, Eliot," announced Cohen; then into the telephone, "Stand by to receive again."

"All ready," buzzed the earphones.

So the switches were thrown once more, and once more came the flash and the ozone.

"One, two, three, four," counted Cohen.

Endicott stared at the seated thug in the cubicle. As the switches were thrown, an opaque mist seemed to spring from the three coördinate axes, enveloping Red and the chair in a cube of pearly liquid fire. Then as the "one, two, three, four" were counted off, the man dissolved and disappeared, leaving only the chair and an automatic pistol, which appeared suddenly in the vicinity of one of Red's pockets, and clattered to the floor.

"Where is he?" gasped Endicott.

"Headquarters by now," replied Cohen laconically.

"But why did the chair and the pistol stay behind?"

"Because they are metal," explained the other. "For some as yet unexplained reason, this apparatus won't transmit metals. The darn fool took the wrong chair. He'll get an awful bump when he lands up in New Hampshire."

So that was where the headquarters was, somewhere in New Hampshire. Too bad there were no more envelopes. This was an important clue.

To divert Cohen's attention from this slip, Endicott hastily inquired, "But there's lots of iron, and phosphorus, and other metals in the human anatomy. Why don't these get left behind, too?"

"Because they exist in the form of metallic salts. This machine will transmit metallic salts, although not metals. Your turn next, Eliot; and take a *wooden* chair, if you don't want a bump. Oh, by the way, you had better leave your watch, and pocket-knife, and garters, and jewelry, and so forth, outside. They will be mailed to you. The machine wouldn't do them any good. Look at Red's gat there: the rubber handle-grips, the grease, and the powder from the cartridges have gone with him, and the rest of the gun is here. When you go, all your tooth-fillings will remain here. But we maintain a special dental clinic at head-quarters, for just that purpose."

Dr. Polakowski removed the steel chair and the gat, and obligingly placed a wooden chair in the cubicle; and Eliot Endicott sat down on it, not without considerable misgivings.

HE LOOKED around him for some means of escape, but saw none. He became frantic with terror of the unknown. Had he not just seen the gunman, Red, dissolve into nothing? Now it was about to happen to him.

More for the purpose of stalling for time, than because of any scientific inquisitiveness, Eliot hurriedly said, "Just a minute, Aaron! How can you be sure that some one else will not tune in on this station, and receive a part of me—all mixed up with a bedtime story?" He laughed nervously at his grim humor.

Cohen smiled indulgently. As there was no chance for Eliot to escape, he might just as well humor the attorney.

"There is not a chance in the world. We use a compound wave-length, very similar to that employed in the Hammond torpedo-control. That is to say, we send simultaneously each of the three dimensions on five interrelated wave-lengths, each from a different one of five aërials. Each of our stations picks up on five aërials. When both the sending and the receiving sets are properly tuned, there is no other possible combination of antennæ in the world which could receive the transmittal. In this way, we get a directional effect without using directional antennæ.

"The only harmful possibility, then, is that some one may interfere with us, by sending at the same instant something on the same wave-length as ours. But, as in the Hammond torpedo-control, any third party can interfere with one or two of each of our five groups of waves, without in the least disturbing our system. And, to make assurance doubly sure, we have perfected a polarized ray, obtained in a manner somewhat analogous to that in which Iceland spar polarizes light, which can be received only by a radio of like polarity. So there isn't the slightest chance of a single portion of your anatomy going astray. As a matter of fact, we don't transmit you yourself at all; we merely dissolve into energy every particle which constitutes your body, and then build it up again, atom for atom, at the other end. Quite spooky, I'll admit, but you'll never notice the difference."

This explanation convinced, but did not reassure the attorney.

He nerved himself to the ordeal. If there was no escape, at least he could deprive these criminals of the satisfaction of seeing him cringe. So he sat calmly in the cubicle, with an assumed nonchalance, and with a forced smile on his bloodless face. He looked his executioner squarely in the eye.

Through his brain ran the quotation, "My only regret is that I have but one life to give for my country," and at that he really smiled.

Then the curtains were closed, and he heard the usual formula repeated between the two scientists over the telephone. There came the flash, and the smell, and the pearly fire streaming from the three coördinate axes.

A wave of nausea swept over the young man, but in an instant he felt quite himself again. He shuddered, and shook his head to clear his brain. Still inside the same curtains he was. Apparently nothing had happened. He drew in his breath sharply through his mouth, and experienced an acute pain in one tooth.

The curtains were thrown open, and he stepped out into an entirely different room, a rough-boarded lumber-camp shack. The motor-generator set, the panel, the coils, and the interrupter were quite differently placed than before, and two strange men in smocks were at the controls. The pterodactyl and the gunman Red were standing with them.

The two men in smocks shook hands gravely with the newcomer, but did not offer to introduce themselves.

The dragon clicked sharply three times, whereupon one of the men handed it a slate and slate-pencil with great deference. To Endicott's surprise, the dragon wrote on the slate, pressing it to the floor with one wing-claw and grasping the pencil with the other. The writing looked like some kind of shorthand.

One of the men read the message and then announced, "The King says to take you to the infirmary. Red, you will escort the gentleman."

So the young prisoner was led out of the laboratory into thick and beautiful mountain woods, through which the moonlight filtered. As he surveyed the totally unfamiliar scene around him, it gradually dawned on Eliot Endicott that he had actually been transmitted somewhere away from Boston by that preposterous apparatus. New Hampshire, as mentioned by Cohen, sounded highly plausible.

RED LED him along a little path for a few hundred feet to another shack, at which he knocked. The door was opened by a trained nurse, who seemed to be expecting a patient, for she took Eliot inside at once, without a word to him or his conductor, who promptly departed.

In what was evidently a reception room, she indicated a chair and left him. For a moment he thought of flight. Here he was totally unguarded for the first time since his capture. Then he realized the futility of attempting escape, until he knew more of his whereabouts and of the location and numbers of the enemy. The camp might well be surrounded by insurmountable fences and patrolled by military guards, for all he knew. Furthermore, it behooved him to learn all that he could about this gang before his letter to Helyn led eventually to his rescue, as he believed it, in the natural course of events, must.

His thoughts were interrupted by the entrance of a brisk young man in a white operating coat, who greeted him with, "So you are the famous Eliot Endicott, the man who is expected to break up our organization. I have read about you in the Boston papers. We are very glad you are going to join us instead. My name is Dr. Victor Chapin."

As he arose to shake hands, Endicott replied, "But I am most decidedly not going to join your confounded organization. Why does every one assume that I am?"

"Because you are," asserted Chapin, smiling. "All I've got to do is to give you a new-soul, and you'll be one of us. Quite a simple operation, I assure you."

"What in the name of Heaven do you mean? I always thought that I was born with a soul."

"Well, you weren't; not this kind of soul. We who used to be mere humans distinguish them as new-souls. We breed them in the laboratories here, and so I ought to know. However, that can wait until later. We must first repair your teeth. You left all your fillings behind in Boston, I believe."

"But tell me about this 'souls' business."

"That can wait," asserted the young doctor peremptorily. "I really ought not to have mentioned it. We'll attend to your teeth now. Your soul, later."

"You do dental work at this time of night?"

"Yes," replied the doctor. "We run two shifts. Our army is growing so rapidly that it taxes our facilities to the utmost to do all the dental work, and to install all the new-souls. You'll find the dentistry quite painless, as we use oxygen and nitrous-oxide analgesia."

He pushed a button and another white-coated man entered.

"Fix Mr. Endicott's teeth," directed Dr. Chapin sharply.

The other doctor bowed obsequiously to him.

"Just a moment," objected Eliot Endicott. "Will they be doing anything about my soul while I am under this anæsthetic, having my teeth fixed?"

"No," Dr. Chapin assured him. "On my word of honor."

So Endicott went away with the dentist. He didn't like the looks of this new man, who somehow was not quite human. In fact only Cohen and Chapin seemed human, of all the members of the organization whom he had yet met. The rest were more in a class with the pterodactyl. There was something uncannily animal about them all. Red, Boris, Frank, the other gunmen,

Dr. Polakowski, the two laboratory men on this end, the little trained nurse, and now the dentist. All of them were robots, or so it seemed to Eliot. Cohen and Dr. Chapin were two human beings, directing an army of robots or televoxes.

The teeth-filling was uneventful. A rather pretty but robot-like nurse—not the one who had met him at the door—administered the anæs-thetic. He took a couple of deep breaths, and then the doctor removed the nose-clip.

"Aren't you going to fill my teeth?" he asked.

"All over," said the dentist with a smile. "That's the way with oxygen and nitrous-oxide. You don't know that you're going under, or that you are under, or that you're coming out. The King certainly makes use of the best of human inventions. It's a wonder to me that people in the outside world will stand for dentists who don't use analgesia."

ELIOT ENDICOTT got out of the chair a bit bewildered and a bit dizzy. He didn't feel quite himself. He began to wonder if perhaps they hadn't done something to his "soul" while he was under.

The pretty nurse led him away to a private ward in the hospital.

"Dr. Chapin says that you are to live here until you are operated on," she explained.

So he hadn't yet lost, or gained, his soul, or what have you? Greatly relieved, although he had no idea what it all meant, he waved good night to the nurse, shut the door, undressed, put on the pair of hospital pyjamas which he found hanging there, crawled into bed, and soon was fast asleep. Although he tried to concentrate upon his predicament, and to make plans for outwitting his enemies, he was too tired. These efforts served, like counting imaginary sheep, merely to lull him to a disturbed sleep all the more quickly.

His dreams were troubled. During most of them he fled, hand in hand with Helyn Kent, before man-headed pterodactyls, man-headed pigeons, and animal-headed men.

Immediately on awakening the next morning, he rushed to the window. But it was heavily barred, and the view showed merely the hillside above him. No hope either of escape or of information from that quarter.

An interne brought him his breakfast. When he had finished, he dressed and shaved—clean linen and a razor having been provided. Then Red called for him, with a message that Mr. Cohen wished to see him at once at the administration building.

The way led through a beautiful mountain forest, birches and evergreens, beautiful as only New Hampshire forests can be. There was quite a settlement here, he found, built upon a wooded hillside. Through the trees, he could see far off down into the valley, and to the mountains beyond; but everywhere that he gazed, there was nothing except woods. Not a thing to indicate what part of New Hampshire they were in.

The administration building was a newly built shack like the rest, only a bit more pretentious. Red left him at the door, and a stenographer—with the same robot-like, unhuman, expression as the rest—met him there and led him in.

After a short wait in an anteroom, he was admitted to Cohen's office.

His young classmate greeted him as though he were an important business acquaintance, rather than a prisoner.

"Look here!" Endicott blurted out. "Why all this courtesy, and pretense at being decent to me? I'm your enemy and your prisoner."

Cohen smiled indulgently, as he replied, "Old man, you are going to become one of us, whether you like it or not; but we hope, by courtesy, to induce you to join us voluntarily. Our experience shows that the operation is always more successful when voluntarily submitted to."

Endicott smiled a superior smile. The temptation to exhibit his triumph proved too great for his dramatic instinct to withstand.

"Oh, you supermen!" he sneered. "I dropped a letter in the mail-chute on the way through the hall to your laboratory back there in Boston. I did it right under your very eyes. You mentioned New Hampshire—so did I in the letter."

The last wasn't the truth, but it added to his dramatic triumph.

He continued, "Even now my rescuers are on the way here. You rattlesnakes have caught another fanged creature this time!"

Cohen immediately became visibly agitated, which fact added still further to Endicott's triumph.

"To whom was the letter addressed?" he snapped.

"Now wouldn't I be a fool to tell you?" sneered Endicott in reply. "One of your gang would be sent to get it away from her."

" 'Her?' A girl, eh? Your sweetheart, undoubtedly. Well, just watch us make you tell!"

Endicott bit his lip. He ought never have used the word "her!" But he stiffened and said, "You can't make me tell. I'll die first."

"Movie stuff, eh?" laughed Cohen, now calm again. "There are more things in heaven and earth, Eliot, than are dreamt of in your criminal investigations."

He pushed a desk button. The pretty stenographer entered.

"Tell Rajindra Singh to meet me at once in Number Seven. Make it snappy, my dear."

He pushed another desk-button twice. Two robot-like thugs entered.

"Rush this gentleman to laboratory Number Seven, tie him in a chair, and guard him until I get there."

So Eliot Endicott was unceremoniously hustled to another building, struggling futilely in the iron grip of the two man-bodied creatures, and was carefully tied up.

CHAPTER IV

THE INVADERS

A FEW MINUTES later Cohen entered, accompanied by a black-bearded, dark-skinned, turbaned individual with piercing dark eyes.

"Swami Singh," commanded Cohen hurriedly, "get in touch with this man's thoughts instantly. A letter. A letter to a girl, written last night, and now in the mails. I must see it."

Without haste, and yet with steady rapidity, the Hindu pushed a table up to a position beside Endicott's chair, and placed a large crystal globe upon it. Then another table, bearing a complicated arrangement of lenses and electric apparatus, was wheeled up alongside the first table.

Cohen meanwhile brought up a third table, with other machinery, and plugged in cords connected with both. A silver screen was unrolled on the wall before the prisoner, and the room was darkened. A square of light showed on the silver screen.

The Hindu placed one hand on Endicott's forehead, and the other on the crystal globe; and boomed out, "Think of the beautiful girl and of the letter which you wrote her."

Involuntarily the bound man's thoughts flashed to his cousin Helyn, to the letter which he had surreptitiously written in captivity the night before, and to the mail chute in which he had dropped it. Only too late did he realize that it was imperative that he wipe all these thoughts from his mind. Instantly he concentrated on repeating the multiplication table. But it was too late.

"This young man has a strong will," reported Rajindra Singh. "He has shut off his thoughts as with a switch. But not until we were completely *en rapport* with respect to that letter. Observe."

And he nodded toward the screen. Eliot Endicott looked, and was startled to see the features of his cousin Helyn materialize upon it. Forgotten was the multiplication table. Back flashed his thoughts to the letter which he had written her, and suddenly there upon the screen was the letter, going down the chute. The *swami* made an adjustment, and the letter reappeared, jammed together with a lot of others, evidently inside a bag.

"You see," came the voice of Aaron Cohen, "what can be accomplished by combining the ancient wisdom of India with modern science. Observe the linking of a crystal globe, the telepathic powers of a Hindu *swami,* and a stereopticon projector. And now—did you ever see a telautograph, one of those machines that transmit handwriting by electricity? They have them in banks, for train announcers, and for floor to floor communication in hotels. You must have seen them."

Endicott nodded miserably. He felt completely in their power. Why, oh why had he been so foolish as to mention the letter?

As Cohen was speaking, the scene on the silver screen shifted to a long sheet-iron table. The mail bag was dumped out, and there, face up, separate from the others, lay a stamped envelope addressed to "Miss Helyn Kent, Charlesgate Apartments, Cambridge, Massachusetts."

"Now, Eliot, watch the telepathograph, the triumph of modern occult science," announced Cohen.

So saying, he picked up the stylus of his apparatus and made several horizontal scratches with it.

"Now look at the screen," said he.

Endicott looked. The words "Charlesgate Apartments, Cambridge, Massachusetts," on the letter had been neatly ruled out.

Cohen then wrote something rapidly with his stylus; and as he wrote, Endicott was horrified to see the words "Jones Lumber Camp, Bartlett, New Hampshire," appear, as though by magic, on the letter upon the screen.

Just as the address changing was completed, a uniformed postal employee appeared on the scene, and began sorting out the mail on the sheet-metal table. Rajindra Singh swiftly switched off the projection apparatus, and pulled up the window shades.

"The letter will now come to us," asserted Cohen. "Your girl will never give it to the authorities, or, even know what has become of you. We thank you for boasting about the letter. It is your *third* tactical mistake."

"You devil!" exclaimed the prisoner, straining at his bonds.

But Aaron Cohen only smiled tolerantly down at him.

Endicott's face would have borne the smile, and Cohen's the consternation, if they could only both have realized that this remarkable combination of crystal gazing and stereopticon projection was only speeding the fatal letter all the more rapidly to Helyn Kent, its original addressee.

AFTER Eliot's rage subsided he was untied.

"I really like to have you try to pit your powers against us," remarked his sinister classmate. "You are almost too clever for us. It gives me quite a thrill to oppose you. But you are so very, very indiscreet. Four serious slips have you made thus far. First, you bolted your office door on the inside. Secondly, you forgot that rattlesnakes hunt in pairs. Thirdly, you boasted about the letter. And fourthly, you mentioned that you had sent it to your girl."

"I only said 'a' girl!" interrupted Endicott.

"All right, a girl, then," continued Cohen. "Well, anyway, you made the four slips, and but for all of them you might have won over us. I want you to practice a little more discretion, for you are destined to fill an important position in our organization."

"Oh, cut it out, Aaron," remonstrated the exasperated Endicott. "I'm not going to join you, no matter what you offer."

"We'll see," replied Cohen enigmatically. "I am beginning to think of a rather good plan to make you want to join us."

Then the captive was sent back under guard to his room in the hospital. Lunch was served him there. After lunch magazines were brought him.

Also writing materials, with a brief note:

> I thought you might wish to write some more letters.
> AARON COHEN.

He tore up the note indignantly; what was the use of writing a letter here? The magazines afforded him but little amusement, for he spent most of his time worrying over his predicament. And finally a new worry came and quite blotted out all others, for it suddenly occurred to him that Helyn was no longer safe, now that his captors knew her identity and her Cambridge address.

After supper Cohen called briefly. He brought the morning papers, with the mention of Endicott's disappearance marked with blue pencil.

It was a blow to the assistant district attorney's pride to see how little attention had been paid to this, until Cohen pointed out what would have occurred to Endicott in a moment: "The authorities have evidently suppressed the stories. They probably have a clue. We must step warily from now on."

This seemed logical to Endicott also, but Cohen threw a new chill over him by continuing, "It may interest you to know that we have secured your report. Stole it right out from under the very nose of the district attorney, after he had taken it from the safe behind your bookcases. A newspaper reporter named Larrabee is on your trail, but we have him shadowed. If anything more turns up, I'll let you know. Good evening."

"Think of that letter!" the Swami commanded the bound man.

So the criminal organization had won all along the line! Endicott fell asleep that night worrying for the safety of Helyn.

The next morning after breakfast he was summoned to the administration building again.

After a short wait he was escorted into the office of Aaron Cohen, who announced, "I have a special honor for you. You are to be presented at court."

Thereupon he was conducted into the most pretentious room which he had yet seen in this woodland camp. The rough slab walls were completely covered with gorgeous oriental tapestries, and the floor with expensive Persian rugs. On a raised dais, at the end farthest from the entrance, squatted the huge slate-gray pterodactyl, which Endicott had seen before. But on each side of it was a strange new creature.

On its right stood a jet black ant, the size of a horse. Yet, except for its size, it was identically like the little black ants with which the people of this earth are familiar. On the top of its head, held there by straps, was a microphone similar to those used in broadcasting studios. Beside the microphone was a radio loud-speaker. Both were wired to the ant's antennæ and to certain other apparatus carried by a belt about the creature's thorax.

On the left of the gray flying dragon was a scarlet throne, on which sat a gorgeously beautiful woman, gowned in a form-fitting robe of royal blue velvet. And such a form! Never had Eliot Endicott seen such a perfect, such a ravishing feminine figure. On her golden hair was perched a gold crown set with sapphires.

Her face and arms were golden, too, rather than the to-be-expected pink; and, as Endicott studied them more closely, he saw that this was due to a thick short yellow fur which covered her entire skin. Yet so perfect were her features that their furry covering would have gone wholly unnoticed but for its golden color. Set in the golden face were eyes of a blue so deep that they nearly matched her dress and the sapphires of her crown.

"Your majesties," announced Cohen, bowing low and deferentially, "may I present Eliot Endicott, Esq., Assistant United States District Attorney, of Boston, Massachusetts?"

Endicott bowed politely, with his eyes glued to the face of the queen.

His first thought had been, "What a strange triumvirate!" But this was quickly superseded by a fascination for the golden one.

And then she spoke, in a tinkling silver voice, like the noise of the wood thrush of those same New Hampshire mountains, a note so exquisitely beautiful that it almost causes pain.

The enthrallment of Eliot Endicott grew as he listened to that siren voice.

"We are honored," she said. "So you are to join our band, Mr. Endicott? We welcome you."

He was too enchanted to refuse.

"We can use your training," boomed from the loud-speaker of the ant, in guttural tones.

The gray pterodactyl said nothing, but merely stared at the young man with unblinking eyes.

ENDICOTT was led from the room.

"Who are they?" he demanded as soon as he was outside.

"I rather thought you would be interested," Cohen replied. "The dragon is Boomalayla, King of Yat. The antman is Doggo, formerly a Formian of Cupia, but now of Yat as well. The lady is Quivven the Goldenflame, a Princess of Vairkingia."

"And what the deuce are Yat, and Cupia, and Vairkingia? I have never heard of them."

Cohen laughed.

"You wouldn't be expected to," he replied. "Those are all countries of the planet Venus. The King, Boomalayla, longed for new worlds to conquer, but being hemmed in by powerful enemies on the two continents each side of Yat, he picked up the Earth as being a simpler proposition. So he and Doggo and Quivven came down here."

"But how could they get here from Venus—assuming that you aren't stringing me?" asked Endicott.

"They knew the secret of the wireless transmission of matter. I helped on this end, having first had the good fortune to get in touch with them by a special long-distance radio of my own design. In fact, the enterprise of their conquest of the Earth was largely my idea. As a reward for my assistance, I stand first in power beneath the Great Three. A sort of prime minister."

"It sounds to me," the other commented, "for all the world like the ravings of an opium-dream; and yet those creatures are not known on Earth; it may well be true. The evidence certainly points that way."

"You remind me," laughed Cohen, "of the hayseed who gazed for a long time at a giraffe in a circus, and then sadly shook his head and remarked, 'There ain't no sech animile.'"

Endicott was then returned to his quarters, and was left with his magazines again.

CHAPTER V

TO DISPOSE OF A CLUE

AARON COHEN IN person visited the post office at Bartlett that morning to get the mail, but the redirected letter from Eliot Endicott to Helyn Kent hadn't yet arrived. He came again in person for the afternoon mail, but still the coveted letter was not among those in his box. So he made bold to inquire of the postmaster.

"You haven't seen a letter addressed to Miss Helyn Kent, Jones Lumber Camp, have you?"

"Sure I have," replied the official. "But I thought the address was a mistake, though, so I give it to Miss Kent herself. She was in here just a minute ago."

"Well, you pulled a boner!" asserted Cohen positively, never dreaming that this could be the very Miss Kent for whom the letter had been originally intended. "Any Miss Kent whom you may have around here is not the one at our camp. I don't see why you postmasters are so officious. You're all the time sending letters to where you think folks are, instead of trusting to the sender of the letter to know what he's about. Where does this local Miss Kent live?"

"Up at Morton's," replied the postmaster. "And I'm awfully sorry, Mr. Jones, that it happened."

"You ought to be," snarled Cohen, hastening out the door.

Jumping into his expensive foreign runabout, he fairly flew up the road toward Morton's. On the way, he passed a young man trudging along the same road, but took no particular note of him, so intent was he on one special guest.

Presently he overtook a Ford beach wagon driven by a young girl. She was alone in the car.

"Oh, Miss Kent!" he sang out.

The girl looked back, then stopped her car. Cohen came to a stop just behind her, hopped out, and hastened to the side of the beach wagon.

He was handsome and quite evidently a gentleman. His runabout bespoke respectability. And he acted as though he were acquainted with her.

"Yes?" she asked tentatively.

"Miss Kent," said he, "you have just received a letter—"

"What do *you* know of that letter?" she demanded.

Instantly he had an intuition that she must be the Miss Kent for whom the letter had been intended. By some remarkable mischance, all the trouble which he had taken in order to read-dress Eliot Endicott's letter, by occult means, so that it would be forwarded to Bartlett, New Hampshire, had merely resulted in the letter going more speedily and directly to its original addressee than it would have gone, if he had let it alone.

Aaron Cohen was in a quandary. Had this girl yet read the letter? If so, the readdressing might give her—or the authorities—some clue as to the whereabouts of young Endicott; and Aaron's inquiries would serve as further clues. But if she hadn't yet read the letter, he must by all means continue the pretense of the existence of a girl of the same name at his camp, in order to get the letter away from Helyn unread. So first he must find out how much she knew.

These thoughts raced through his mind in an instant, and he continued, "Miss Kent, have you read that letter?"

If not, he could claim that his anxiety was due to its being a very confidential communication for his alleged Helyn Kent.

But she had read the letter, and had been thoroughly shocked by its contents; so she now became suspicious and apprehensive.

"Who are you?" she asked, drawing away from him. " And what do you know about any letter?"

So she had read the letter! That was instantly evident. Well, then, he must change his tactics; and quickly, too.

"I know a great deal, my dear young lady," he suavely replied, "for I am an operative from the Department of Justice. Eliot Endicott—"

She started visibly at the name.

Cohen smiled, and went on, "Endicott left another note, which has fallen into the Department's hands. It began with the words. 'I have written Helyn—' and was never finished. The Department at once ascertained that you are the only known person of that name in his circle of friends. The authorities located you at Bartlett. I happened to be in the vicinity, so they phoned me and explained the situation, and here I am. Very simple, isn't it? We must act quickly, if we would save your friend, who is in the hands of a band of desperate criminals. Does the letter contain any information as to where the young man is?"

IT SOUNDED plausible enough. But some intuition warned Helyn to be careful. She did not want to offend this nice young man if he were truly a Secret Service agent; neither did she want to take any chances.

So she replied most disarmingly. "The letter does contain what I believe to be important information. I was hurrying home to show it to father, when you overtook me. We are staying at Morton's, as you probably know. It's nearer than town; and, as you say, we must act quickly. Won't you come along? You can use the Morton phone, and father can undoubtedly help you with some ideas. He is quite a clever lawyer."

Cohen pretended to be slightly offended, though still gracious.

"I can see that you don't quite trust me," said he, "and you are very wise not to. In an emergency like this, I wouldn't trust anybody myself, until he had conclusively proved himself to be an operative of the Department."

He paused for a moment, studying her face with a quizzical smile. Then, "Would you like to see my credentials?"

She murmured some kind of an apology, which he took for an assent.

"This will convince you, I am sure," said he.

Reaching into one of his pockets, he produced a small object which he held up to her. Eagerly she leaned forward out of the car, to see what it was. But it seemed to be merely something oval and white, about the size of a bird egg.

Puzzled, she raised her eyes inquiringly to his; and at just that instant, he pushed the round white object under her nose, and crunched the capsule between his thumb and fingers.

Without a sound, Helyn Kent pitched forward unconscious out of her beach wagon, and Cohen caught her as she fell.

Then Lawrence Larrabee came plodding up the hill behind them.

CHAPTER VI

HOT ON THE TRAIL

THE MOMENT THAT Helyn Kent succumbed to the powerful anæsthetic contained in the capsule which the prime minister of the "Great Three" had squeezed under her nose, Cohen caught her in his arms, thrust her back into her beach wagon, and jumped in beside her.

When Lawrence Larrabee reached the spot, on his trudging hike toward Morton's, the beach wagon was already disappearing in a cloud of dust up the road. Larry passed Cohen's runabout, standing deserted in the middle of the road, and trudged on. He mildly wondered what that car was doing there, and what had become of its occupant—being a reporter, it was natural for him to wonder about things—but he was far too engrossed with his quest for the missing Eliot Endicott, and incidentally the beautiful girl whom he had seen and admired on the train, to waste much thought on such an apparently irrelevant phenomenon as a foreign-built roadster standing deserted in the middle of a New Hampshire woods road.

The Morton camp turned out to be quite a palatial establishment—not at all the mere log cabin which Larry had expected. He rang the bell and inquired for Miss Kent, only to be told that she wasn't at home. He felt a distinct shock of disappointment.

He felt aggrieved, but of course it was natural that she should be out—to him. Undoubtedly she had noticed his interest in her on the train, and had resented it. She might even have recognized him in the post office that afternoon, and again resented his interest. Probably she had seen him approaching the camp, and so had given orders to the servants that he was not to be admitted.

He mumbled something and turned away from the door.

Yet it was imperative that he see her, and at once! For she and he possessed between them all the clues that there were as to what had become of Eliot Endicott. But how was he to go about seeing her?

There suddenly came over him the futility of his entire trip to Morton's. He realized now that he had tramped all this way, not on the trail of the missing assistant U.S. attorney, as he had kidded himself into believing, but rather merely for an excuse to make the acquaintance of Helyn Kent.

What he ought to have done was to have communicated at once with his paper, the *Post*, and thus scooped the other papers before the Kents got word to the authorities, and the authorities gave out a statement.

But now that he was here, would it not be better to cooperate with the Kents—if he could persuade them to coöperate with him—and thus be in touch with whatever moves they might make? Besides, this would give him a chance to meet Helyn. It was not hard for him to convince himself.

So he fished in his pocket for a piece of paper and scratched the following message:

> My dear Miss Kent:
> Please pardon the intrusion, but I am on the trail of Eliot Endicott. I happen to know, never mind how, that you have some valuable information as to his whereabouts. So have I. Can't we pool our information? We must act quickly, if we would save him.
> Sincerely yours,
> Lawrence Larrabee.

Then he once more approached the door, rang the bell, and handed the note to the maid.

"Please give this note to Miss Kent," said he.

"But I told you once that she is out," replied the servant.

"Well, give her this," said Larry, "and I'll bet she won't be out for long."

"Do you want I should give it to her when she gets back?" persisted the maid, quite exasperatingly, it seemed to him.

"I want you should give it to her right now!" mimicked Larry, a bit nettled.

A masculine voice was heard in the hall, saying, "What's all this disturbance about?"

"Please, sir," said the maid, turning away from the door, "it's a young gentleman as has a note for Miss Helyn, and insists that she's in, when I tell him she's out."

Blackstone Kent appeared in the doorway. His brows contracted as he saw and recognized Larry.

"So!" he bellowed. "So it's the young cub who followed us around on the train. May I ask if you are acquainted with my daughter?"

"N-n-no," stammered Larry, "but—"

"Then get out!" interrupted Kent.

"But this is important," insisted the reporter. "Your daughter got a letter—"

"Well, she's not going to get any more," Kent again interrupted.

And taking the note from the hand of the grinning maid, he threw it in Larry's face, and slammed the door.

Larry could have kicked himself. Where was his reportorial instinct? Where was the finesse which had secured him many an interview from persons who were even more forbidding than Blackstone Kent? Well, at least he still had his persistence. He would now do what he ought to have done in the first place.

So he readdressed the note, to Mr. Kent, and for the third time rang the bell.

But Kent surprised him by answering the door in person.

Before Larry Could recover from this unexpected appearance, the door had been slammed once more, and the note remained still undelivered.

It would do no good to ring and ring; he realized that. So he added a postscript to the note, stuffed it under the door, and turned sadly away. It read:

> P. S.—When you get over your tantrum and have read this note, if you are interested in finding Eliot Endicott, phone me at the hotel in Bartlett.
>
> L.L.

Then Larry tramped back to town in the gathering dusk.

On the way, he met the foreign-built runabout. Cohen was in it this time, driving toward Morton's.

"Careless of him to have parked in the middle of the road like that back there," thought Larry, as he hurried on.

MEANWHILE Aaron Cohen had been busier than ever before in his eventful life. Just beyond the spot where he had administered the knock-out drops to Helyn Kent, there was a side-road leading to the right. Down this, Cohen turned the beach wagon, with the unconscious girl lying crumpled beside him on the seat. By devious wood-paths, known only to himself, he speedily reached his alleged lumber camp, where he turned Helyn over to the hospital authorities.

But first he searched her pockets, and found the incriminating letter. Good! She had not yet shown it to any one. What a narrow escape! Now he had the letter, and young Endicott's sweetheart as well. Quite a haul for one afternoon!

Then he drove the beach wagon to the garage of the lumber camp, where he ordered its complete and immediate dismantling; so as to leave not a single trace to serve as an incriminating clue. One of the garage mechanics drove him, in another car, back to where he had left his own runabout.

There was only one flaw in the whole situation. The postmaster knew that Cohen had set out to follow Helyn Kent and get from her a letter which Cohen had claimed was meant for some one at his own camp. So it was probable that when Helyn failed to show up, and her family became alarmed and began to make inquiries, the postmaster would tell what he knew, which would result in Aaron's being questioned.

There was but one thing to do: brazen it out. So he sped on to Morton's.

Blackstone Kent answered the door in somewhat of an ill-humor, as he expected to find there the same fresh young man who had been annoying him. But when he saw that it was a handsome and distinguished-looking stranger, evidently a gentleman, the lawyer was much mollified.

"What can I do for you?" he asked in his most affable manner.

"Mr. Kent?" inquired Cohen.

"Yes."

"I am Washington Jones, proprietor of the Jones Lumber Camp near here," Cohen explained.

The two men shook hands.

The pretended Mr. Jones then continued, "Mr. Kent, there is a girl at my camp with the same name as your daughter. A very important letter arrived for her this afternoon at the Bartlett post office."

At the mention of "letter," some subconscious idea tried to make contact in Blackstone Kent's mind—but it failed.

Meanwhile Cohen was saying, plausibly enough, "The postmaster being acquainted with your daughter, and never having heard of *my* Miss Kent, gave the letter to your daughter. Is your daughter here?"

"She ought to be by now," replied Kent, "but she's not yet got back from town."

"Strange!" commented Cohen. "For the postmaster told me that she had left the office, bound for here. Well, anyway, when she does return, would you mind sending one of your men right over to my camp with the letter, as it's very important?"

"Won't you step inside and wait, Mr. Jones?" invited Kent hospitably. He was rather taken by this young stranger.

"Thank you, no," replied Cohen, "although I realize that I am putting you to a lot of trouble by having you send the letter over, instead of my waiting here for it. The fact is, I am due at an important business conference back at my office at the lumber camp. So if you would be so good—"

"No trouble at all, I assure you," boomed the lawyer. "Drop around and see us again some time, when you are not so busy."

The two men shook hands, and Aaron Cohen sped away again in his roadster, back to camp. All this time Larry's note to Blackstone Kent lay unnoticed on the doorstep.

Back at the Jones lumber camp, Cohen found that he had unintentionally told one iota of truth to Kent, for a conference was actually in progress.

Dr. Chapin had given to the triumvirate—Boomalayla the winged dragon, Doggo the antman, and Quivven the golden Princess—a brief report of Helyn's capture; and the three were not altogether satisfied with the situation. So Cohen found himself called to explain and justify. He could talk to Quivven and Doggo, but he was forced to use Porovian shorthand with the huge pterodactyl, which slowed up, matters considerably, especially as the pterodactyl was the final authority.

Cohen's explanations, however, were accepted. The triumvirate approved readily enough his capture of Helyn, both for the purpose of securing the letter, and for the further purpose of holding her as a hostage for the young assistant district attorney's good behavior. They approved of the tactics which he had pursued to throw Helyn's father off the scent.

But they did not share his confidence that no one else than Helyn had read the letter. Also Chapin had told them something of Blackstone Kent, how he was one of the keenest-minded criminal lawyers of Massachusetts. Now they were likely to have him on their trail, which likelihood boded trouble.

"Leave him to me," asserted Cohen overconfidently.

But the three were not so cocksure.

"All right," exclaimed Cohen, "let's send for Rajindra Singh, and see who's right."

THE THREE nodded approval, so the young man stepped briskly to a wall-telephone and issued some hurried orders. Then the four of them left the throne-room and walked through the evening shadows to Laboratory No. 7.

Dr. Chapin, Swami Singh and Miss Kent were already there, when they arrived. The girl was seated rigidly in a chair, and the Hindu was making passes across her forehead and in front of her eyes, with both his hands.

"She sleeps," he announced, as they entered. "She will now tell the truth. What do you wish me to ask her?"

Cohen shot a glance, half of malice, half of anticipated triumph, at the doctor. Then pulled a folded letter from one pocket, and handed it to Singh.

"Ask her what this is," said he.

The Hindu repeated the question.

"What is this?" said he, holding it before her.

"A letter," replied Helyn, in the dull voice of one talking in sleep.

"What is it about?" persisted Singh.

In spite of her trance, the girl became agitated.

"My cousin, Eliot, is in trouble. He is in the hands of criminals. He wants me to help him. But I can't. I started home with the letter. But before I could tell father, or any one else, something happened to me. I don't know where I am, but I *must* save Eliot. Please, please help me!"

She turned piteous, pleading, sleepwalker's eyes from one to another of her captors; but their faces remained grim and inexorable.

When she had said the word "cousin," Cohen's looks had fallen. Merely a cousin, was she, and not a sweetheart of young

Endicott! But when she asserted that no one else knew of the letter, he smiled triumphantly.

But the triumvirate were not yet convinced.

Said Quivven the Goldenflame, "Ask her if any one except herself has seen the letter."

So the Swami repeated the question.

"No! No!" wailed their captive. "No one. Too bad! Too bad! I put it in my pocket, as soon as I read it myself in the post office, and hurried home to father. But I never got home. And now no one will ever save Eliot!"

"Bring the globe and the projector," commanded Quivven; and soon the room was darkened, and Rajindra Singh stood with one hand on Helyn's forehead, the other on the crystal ball, while all gazed fixedly at the silver movie-screen.

Blurred iridescent clouds swirled across it like the reflections in rippled water. Then gradually the surface calmed, and a picture pieced itself together, the picture of a smoky room filled with men.

"The lobby of the Bartlett Hotel," announced Cohen. "What can that have to do with—"

"Sh!" admonished Quivven. "Watch."

On the screen, one of the men arose from his chair, threw his cigarette into a spittoon, and started up the stairs. The scene shifted and followed him. Up the stairs he went, and down the corridor to a door, which he opened. Switching on the light, he passed inside.

Helyn Kent was watching him with a fixed intent gaze, her poor drugged mind struggling to recollect his identity.

Cohen noticed this and suddenly asked, "Miss Kent, you know that man. Who is he?"

The picture swirled and blurred. The girl shuddered and rubbed one hand across her eyes. The screen became clear and vacant.

"Where am I?" murmured Helyn, awakening.

"You've broken the spell," the black-bearded Hindu whispered reproachfully to Cohen.

"Then put her back under, as quickly as you can," snapped Cohen.

But Dr. Chapin held up his hand, saying, "That's all her health will permit for to-night."

At a nod and a click of approval from Boomalayla, he picked up the bewildered girl in his arms, and strode from the room.

This gave Cohen just the time needed to recover his poise. When the triumvirate turned their faces to him again, he was once more master of the situation.

"There's a complication here which must be investigated at once," he announced. "I'm going to town to find out who that man is, and what he means to Miss Kent, and to Eliot Endicott. Meanwhile Dr. Chapin had better operate at once. Miss Kent must acquire a new-soul, before we run any danger of her sleuth-hound father finding her."

Quivven and Doggo nodded their approval. Boomalayla shrugged his great gray wings. He hadn't heard Cohen's announcement, but the young man's attitude portended action, and the King approved of action.

Soon Cohen was speeding through the night in his powerful roadster. On the seat beside him was the red-haired ape-man. In the rumble seat was another of his thug henchmen, and two pigeons.

CHAPTER VII

RUTHLESS MEASURES

BLACKSTONE KENT, THOUGH a lawyer, was a typical executive go-getter. He acted first, and did his thinking afterward. He believed with Roosevelt: "Better the wrong thing done promptly, than the right thing done too late."

When his daughter Helyn failed to return home, he first called up every one whom she would be likely to visit, and then drove rapidly to town in his car, and sought the chief of police. Meanwhile Larry's note, which would have gone a long way toward solving the mystery of Helyn's disappearance, still lay unnoticed on the Mortons' doorstep.

Aaron Cohen, with his two seeming lumberjacks and the two ordinary-looking pigeons, reached the town of Bartlett ahead of Blackstone Kent. Leaving the men and the birds in the car, Aaron entered the hotel, walked briskly to the desk, and ran his finger down the register. Many of the names were familiar to him. Three men, and a man and wife, were not. He dismissed from consideration the man and wife. This narrowed his choice to three names.

Approaching the clerk, who was seated out in the lobby reading a magazine, he handed him a cigar, and started chatting about the weather, business, and the prospects for the summer tourist trade.

Finally, in the same casual manner, he asked, "By the way, Charley, who's the young fellow with black curly hair, and an Irish look to his face, that's staying with you?"

"Oh, his name's John O'Brien," replied the clerk, "but there's something funny about him, Mr. Jones. I'm not supposed to let on to any one, but it's all right, seeing it's you, sir, for I know you won't let it get any further. This evening, when he comes in, he says to me, 'Now don't tell any one else, but if Blackstone Kent—'"

Cohen started at the name, but instantly steeled his face to an expressionless mask, as Charley continued, " 'should telephone and inquire for a Mr. Larrabee, please call *me* to the phone.'"

At the word "Larrabee," Cohen started again, but only internally, for he was prepared for something like this, and so his face remained expressionless.

Why, "Laraby" was the name which Jackson had telegraphed from Rockingham Junction! Pigeons had reported that the reporter Larrabee had been in the Federal Building when the packet had been stolen from the office of the district attorney. Pigeons had listened in on Larrabee's conversation with the editor of the Boston *Post*.

Jackson, one of the Boston members of the organization, had been dispatched to follow Larrabee as far as Rockingham Junction, where the reporter had given him the slip and supposedly returned to Boston. Larrabee was known to be on the trail of the missing Eliot Endicott. He was apparently the same young man whom the tapping of Helyn Kent's subconscious mind had thrown on the screen in Laboratory No. 7. Here he was, at their very doorstep, and—what was even more serious— expecting a call from Helyn's father!

This situation required quick action.

Yet Cohen lingered on. He casually inquired about the two other names which he had read in the hotel register. One turned out to be a drug drummer, middle-aged and fat. The other, a noted entomologist, with a long white beard. Cohen pondered the latter's profession, then dismissed them both from consideration.

Nonchalantly he sauntered out of the hotel, and rushed to his parked car, which he then proceeded to drive around the block and into an alley. He knew, from the register, that Larrabee occupied room 31, and from familiarity with the hotel was aware that room 31 was second floor rear. There was a light in only one second floor rear room.

A hurried whispered consultation ensued, and then one of the pigeons fluttered upward in the darkness, to perch for a moment on the sill of the lighted window, and then return. Cohen drew a flash light, and turned its beam on the bird; which had alighted on the ground beside him.

"Is he there?" he asked.

The bird nodded decidedly.

"Is he armed?"

The bird shook its head.

"Any one with him?"

Again the bird gave a negative answer.

"Up and get him, men," commanded Cohen. "One of you pigeons fly to the sill again, and bring me word if anything goes wrong. The other of you pigeons go on guard at the one end of the alley. I'll watch the other end."

LAWRENCE LARRABEE, tired and disgusted, had decided to go to bed. Acting on one of his famous hunches, he took out of his pocket the envelope, which had enclosed Eliot Endicott's letter to Helyn Kent. This envelope he slid underneath the towel which served as a cover for the top of the bureau.

He was then about to undress, when he noticed a pigeon, fluttering for a moment on his window sill. Strange for a bird to be out at this time of night! But perhaps it had been disturbed from its sleep somewhere in the vicinity.

Then he recalled the pigeons who had stolen the packet from the Federal Building, and those who had spied on him in the editor's office at the Boston *Post*.

He looked once more toward the open window, but the bird

was gone. For several minutes he stood watching the window, and puzzling over the occurrence. Then he walked ruminatively over to the window and looked out.

All was dark below, but there seemed to be a man standing at the further end of the alley. Larry leaned far out, to get a better look.

Then suddenly, without warning, a hand was clapped across his mouth, an arm was hooked around his neck, and he was hauled out onto a shed roof just below his window.

Biting and struggling and trying to shout for help, he was forced down onto the roof, where he was promptly bound, gagged, and blindfolded. The last thing that he saw was that a bird was fluttering around the head of the man at the end of the alley, and that the man turned and came toward them.

Then he was lowered off the roof by one pair of strong arms into another, and was carried writhing and struggling to a parked runabout, where he was dumped unceremoniously into the rumble seat. Everything was hurriedly removed from his pockets, and then the car was off and away, one man crouched in the rumble seat beside him, and two others in front.

Larry's hands were not very tightly tied. In the darkness, he groped about behind him, until he happened to feel his own penknife, which must have dropped out of his pocket before his captors searched him. The man beside him wasn't paying much attention, except to hold Larry's head down in his lap. So Larry cautiously, and with as little motion as possible, started sawing through his cords. What little motion there was, was lost in the vibration of the car.

At last he felt that his bonds were all so loosened that, given an even break, he could shake them off at a moment's notice. Now to wait for the said break!

As they droned along through the darkness, there suddenly came a brilliant light, discernible to Larry, even through his bandage. Two differently pitched horns blared at each other. The runabout skidded violently and lurched far over toward

Larry's side, throwing him into a sitting posture out of his captor's lap, and precipitating his captor to the floor of the rumble seat. The runabout slewed into almost a full stop. Larry snatched off his blindfold, stood erect, and jumped.

A few yards further on, the runabout came to a grinding standstill.

"We just squeaked by!" exclaimed Cohen. "That car was sure going hell bent for election! All right, back there, Red?"

Red picked himself up off the floor of the rumble seat.

"No, sir!" he shouted. "That prisoner has fell out!"

With an ejaculation of dismay, Cohen snatched up his flash light and leaped out of the car. His two lumberjacks followed.

The wheel marks showed where they swerved almost into a deep ditch beside the road; and then out again.

"That's where he fell, sir," announced Red.

"Are you sure it was this side he fell on?"

"Yes, sir."

Thick scrub oaks lined the road at this point, but there was not a sound of any fugitive crashing through them.

Sending one man down the ditch in each direction, Cohen stood where he was, and flashed his light first one way and then the other, but Lawrence Larrabee was nowhere to be seen.

Headlights appeared on the road ahead.

"If anything's happened to him, we can't afford to be seen here!" exclaimed Cohen. "Come on!"

So the three leaped into the car and were off in an instant. But as soon as the other auto had passed them, they turned quickly around, and hurried back to renew their search.

BOTH ditches were traversed for some distance in both directions. The lights of their runabout had illuminated the road far ahead of them when they had stopped, and now lighted it for an equal distance the other way. The woods on both sides were too thick to be penetrated without considerable noise. The car which had just passed them had not stopped to pick up any one. For all that they knew, Larry was still securely bound, gagged and blindfolded, and they had found no loose ropes or handkerchiefs in their search.

Their victim had apparently vanished into thin air!

Disgusted and not a little apprehensive, Aaron Cohen called in his forces and drove on to camp.

On arriving there, he roused Dr. Chapin out of bed.

"Did you operate on Helyn Kent?" he asked.

"Did you find out whether she had shown any one that letter?" countered the doctor.

"I'm in command here, Chapin," replied Cohen sternly. "Answer my question."

"No," admitted the doctor. "I thought that she was too weak after your drug and Rajindra's monkey business."

"Could she stand it now?"

"Possibly."

"Could she stand it, if she had to?"

"Well, y-e-s, if she had to."

"Then operate. Operate immediately. Events are moving swiftly, and so we've got to move swiftly. Our whole dream of empire is at stake."

"The letter—"

"Damn the letter! You operate."

"Yes, sir."

Cohen strode out, and went to bed. No need to alarm the triumvirate until morning.

He slept longer than usual, and no one disturbed him.

CHAPTER VIII

ROBOTS AND NEW-SOULS

EARLY IN THE morning Eliot Endicott was summoned before Quivven the Goldenflame. He went, resolved to pretend to fall in with the plans of his captors, and thus to learn as much as possible of their intentions. But when he was ushered into the presence of the golden beauty, her loveliness eclipsed his high resolve. From then on, although he still believed himself to be merely dissembling, an impartial observer of his inner thoughts would have been hard put to determine whether Eliot was deceiving Quivven, or was deceiving himself.

As he entered the throne room and bowed low before the Princess, she smiled down on him and graciously extended one jeweled hand. Seizing it in his, the young man dropped on one knee, and gallantly kissed her hand.

"Arise, Sir Eliot," said she, dimpling with mingled pleasure and amusement. "I like the customs of your planet."

Her voice had the note of another world in it, although her English was perfect.

Endicott arose, still holding her hand, and gazed adoringly into her deep blue eyes. She met his look squarely, with a smile on her lips. And she did not withdraw her hand.

"Come," said, she. "I'm going to show you our establishment."

Then, hand in hand, she led him out of the building.

As they walked along together through the dewy New Hampshire woodland morning, she said in her tinkling silver voice, "I am so glad that you are to join us, Eliot Endicott, for

you are so unlike the other earth-men whom I have met. You
are the first man on this planet whom I really care to know.
That is, to know very well. We are going to have a lot of fun
together, you and I, Eliot Endicott."

Did she really mean it, or was she just flattering him for a
purpose? The young man neither knew nor cared. It was enough
just to be walking beside this strange exotic creature in the fresh
summer morning, and to hold her warm little hand, and listen
to her silver voice. The spell of another world was on him.

"And now," she continued, "I am going to show you how we
are rapidly binding to our cause hundreds, yes, thousands, of
your fellow countrymen."

THEY entered a building where a number of young men in
smocks—professional-looking men—were already at work.
One was putting slices of beef through a meat-grinder screwed
to the end of a work-bench. As the hamburg filled one small
graniteware tray after another, other young men carried the
trays out of the room. On a table near by was a grayish naked
human corpse face down by the side of which, perched on a
high stool, there sat one of the men, with butterfly net in hand,
intently watching the corpse's head.

"That man!" gasped Endicott, dropping Quivven's hand, and
indicating the dead body. "Did you folks kill him?"

"Oh, no," she replied. "He died a natural death. Men must
die, you know, so that their souls may live."

"I've heard this talk of souls or new-souls before," Endicott
blurted out. "What does it mean?"

"All in good time. All in good time," Quivven soothed him.
"That's what I'm showing you now."

Along the walls of the room were shelves containing many
small, fine-meshed cages. Quivven led him over to the shelves.
Each cage contained two brown moths, about an inch in length.

"Souls," stated the golden Princess.

"What do you mean?" gasped Endicott in horror.

"Simply that these are souls," explained Quivven, with an impatient patience in her tone. "We breed them here."

"Breed them? Good Heavens! Of course I know the superstition that the human soul goes into a moth when a man dies, but surely you can't breed souls by just breeding moths! Souls are God-given and are placed in each man at birth. They are not tangible things, to be bred in a laboratory."

"Ah, my friend," replied Quivven, with her quaint foreign accent, "there is more to that superstition than you realize. Years ago on the planet Poros—Venus, you Earth-folk call it—the continent of Whoomangia was a desert jungle, inhabited by all sorts of strange and ferocious beasts, warring upon each other. Then, so tradition relates, there came a man named Namllup, probably from some other continent across the boiling seas, although tradition has it that he rose from the ground fully formed.

"Namllup discovered that the grub, the maggot of a certain rare species of moth, if inserted by a simple operation at the base of the brain of an animal, would immediately give that animal a human, or even superhuman, intelligence. Different species react differently. So Namllup started in to breed these moths. Producing moth-larvæ in ever increasing quantities, he gave 'souls,' as he called them, to the animals of the continent, commencing with the tamer and smaller varieties, and invoking their aid to capture those a little fiercer and wilder, and so on, until there was not a soulless creature on all Whoomangia except certain water-reptiles, what you call 'fish,' which he bred in large numbers to feed the hordes of his Whoomangs. Namllup founded the great city of Yat, the capital of Whoomangia, and his Whoomangs built it.

"Why do you Earth-men seem so horrified about it? Why, men like Mr. Cohen and Dr. Chapin usually insist on calling them 'new-souls,' to distinguish them from whatever you Earthlings mean by 'souls.' They are perhaps something quite different; but the new-souls impart to the creature in which they are placed a portion of the collective soul of Whoomangia, obedient to the will of its rulers."

"These grubs aren't souls, they are the very opposite of souls. It sounds like a ghastly dream!" interpolated the young attorney.

"Ah, but it is the truth, my friend, as I well know, for I was the first human being of the planet Poros to be given a new-soul, and thus become a Whoomang. An airplane, carrying Doggo the antman and myself, and one other, landed near Yat, on a flight across the boiling seas. Doggo and I were captured and operated upon, although our companion made his escape. So now the Quivven that was, is no more, for I am a Whoomang."

"Do you mean to say," exclaimed Eliot Endicott, "that the real you is nothing but a little white worm, living at the base of the brain of that beautiful golden body?"

"It is true," she whispered, with averted face; then suddenly smiling up at him quizzically, she ran one soft furry little hand caressingly down his arm, and murmured; "And yet, you like me, don't you, Eliot Endicott?"

He shuddered, hesitated; then with a rush he breathed, "You know I do."

"And you will join us?"

"Gladly," he replied, "if you will be kind to me."

Taking his hand once more in hers, she said, "Come, my friend, and I will show you all."

ONE OF the attendants passed near them, with a large bottle labeled "sugar solution," and an eyedropper, feeding the moths. Another man followed him. Finally the second man stopped at a cage and deftly transferred its inmates to another cage. The emptied cage he then carried away.

"He has found eggs," explained Quivven. "Let us follow him."

So they did. In the next room they saw the man shake out the cage over a black velvet pad. From the debris he carefully selected, with a pair of tweezers, several dozen tiny white spheres, no bigger than pin-heads. These he deposited, about half an inch apart, in one of the trays of hamburg steak, and then placed the tray on one of the shelves.

"John," commanded the golden Princess, "show us the various stages of hatching."

"Yes, your majesty," replied the attendant deferentially. "Here is a tray that has just hatched."

And he indicated one in which some tiny grubs, could be seen wriggling. Successive groups of trays contained larger and larger "new-souls," until they came to the final trays, the little creatures in which were fully half an inch long.

"These are ready for the hospital," said the attendant.

"Thank you," said Quivven graciously. Then to Endicott, "And now I shall show you the hospital."

As they were leaving the breedery, the man who was perched on the high stool beside the corpse made a swoop with his butterfly net, and then deftly removed a fluttering little moth, which he transferred to one of the wall cages.

"A female!" he announced triumphantly.

"That's good," asserted Quivven, half to herself. "We were running a bit short on females."

As they wended their way through the camp toward the hospital, Quivven continued her explanation: "We have a dozen or more employment agencies in each of the principal cities of America, and a radio station in most of these cities. Every day hundreds of men apply for service with us. We select those who are unattached and who have the particular qualifications which we may desire.

"These men are then sent to our nearest radio station, from which they are transmitted here, or to one of a number of other similar establishments, just as you yourself were. On their arrival they are brought to the hospital, supposedly for a physical examination, but actually for an operation. Once in our power they cannot escape, for each of our camps is surrounded by barbed wire and patrolled by guards whose instructions are to shoot at sight, and shoot to kill."

By this time they had reached another building, which they entered. At a word from Quivven, a nurse promptly ushered them into an operating room. An operating room, yes; but what with the bustle and efficiency, and the impersonal attitude toward what was going on, it more closely resembled a Ford assembly shop.

Four surgeons in white gowns stood each under a ceiling floodlight, with a table of instruments and antiseptics beside him. There were four rows of rubber-wheeled operating tables, one row leading up to each of four doctors. Each table contained an unconscious human figure swathed in blankets, and was accompanied by a trim little trained nurse. At a sink at one side of the room was an interne, with several trays of the sort which Eliot had seen in the breedery. From these the interne was extracting fat white grubs with a pair of tweezers. Another interne, standing by the side of the first, was washing off the grubs in some kind of mild antiseptic and placing them one by one in individual white saucers, which were then carried by a nurse to supply the four doctors.

As each motionless human form was wheeled up to one of the operators, he quickly turned it over on its face with the assistance of its attending nurse. Then the nurse passed a wet cotton swab over a shaved spot at the back of the head, the surgeon deftly made an incision and inserted a grub, and the nurse applied a bandage and wheeled the victim away, to make room for another.

And every face in the establishment was the expressionless face of a robot!

ELIOT ENDICOTT shuddered. A huge factory this was for turning our human beings, at the rate of one a minute, day and night, into animals of another world! And to what end?

Quivven saw his look, and the little hand tightened in his. Eliot looked down at her, and forgot his horror.

Then a question suggested itself.

"What do you do with them all?" he asked. "I should think

that this camp would soon be unable to hold them, and that any undue growth of your camp would attract attention."

Quivven replied, "Some of them we send out into the world, subject to call. With some, we man our ever-expanding interests: factories, farms, rumrunners, espionage. Some we employ here in actual lumbering, just to keep up appearances. But, even so, as you have surmised, our army grows faster than we have any immediate use for them; accordingly, we place our surplus men in storage. Come I will show you."

They followed the four lines of operated-on humanity which were being wheeled out of the room. Just outside the door was a desk, at which a nurse sat with pen and record book. By her side stood an interne, examining the cards with which each wheeled-table was tagged.

"Storehouse... Ward 1... Ward 3... Storehouse... Storehouse... Ward 3... Storehouse..." he droned.

"He's sorting them out," Quivven explained. "Ward I is where our important recruits, our specialists, convalesce. Ward 2 is for the women. Ward 3 is for such hunkies as we have immediate use for. Very important individuals, such as you, are cared for in private wards. All the rest go into storage."

They followed the wheeled tables which had been designated for "storehouse," into an operating-room, a larger one, and with more surgeons.

"This is a longer, slower process," explained Quivven. Then turning to a rather elderly man, with a pointed brown beard, she said, "Dr. Ronk, this is Mr. Endicott, a new member."

As the two men shook hands, Eliot studied the face of the other with interest. It was a rather sad face, with large eyes, which seemed to hide behind their animal dullness, a personality of deep-set pain struggling to assert itself.

"Dr. Ronk," said Quivven, "will you please explain the process to Mr. Endicott."

"Delighted," replied the physician in a monotone, leading the way to one of the operating tables.

The operating surgeon was at the moment making an incision in the right forearm of the patient, exposing a large vein and a large artery. Each of these he slit, and inserted in each the glass end of a long rubber tube. The tubes ran to an electric pump, two tanks, and some dials. He started the pump.

"You see," explained Ronk, in a classroom tone, "he is pumping blood out of the median basal vein, and is pumping Chapin-solution into the radial artery. We used to do it the other way around, but we have found that the tissues cleanse more readily this way."

"And what is Chapin-solution?" asked the young man.

"An invention of our own chief surgeon, Dr. Victor Chapin," replied Ronk. "It is normal saline solution and glucose, plus a hormone which, so Dr. Chapin discovered, would completely inhibit the generation of red blood corpuscles in the bone marrow. Also there is added a strong, but temporary, heart stimulant. The result is that the heart of the patient keeps on beating, long enough for us to drain every drop of blood from his body, and to complete the substitution of our colorless inert solution."

HE PAUSED, and stooped to study the flow through one of the glass pipes.

"See!" he announced. "We are getting almost pure solution out now. His circulatory system has been washed almost clean."

"It seems to me," interrupted Eliot Endicott, "that I once read something very much like this in a fantastic story."

"Quite likely," admitted Dr. Ronk, "for we ourselves got the suggestion from just such a story; but only the general broad suggestion, for the details in the story were preposterous. In the story, the blood was pumped out and saved. That would be absurd. The blood mixes with the injected solution, as you see; and furthermore, even if it came out pure, it couldn't possibly keep, for the corpuscles would die. Then, too, no mere internal injection could preserve the body."

"How, then, do you manage to preserve it?" asked the attorney.

"Wait and see," was the tantalizing reply.

Several minutes later, the doctor who was in charge of this particular patient, stopped the pump, withdrew the tubes, and painted the wound with a small brush.

Dr. Ronk explained. "We have to seal the cuts, for there are no red corpuscles left to coagulate—or, as you would call it, to form a scab—even if we used adrenalin."

The body was then wheeled away, and another patient brought up. Dr. Ronk, Quivven and Endicott followed the first body. The nurse strapped some apparatus to the left forearm, the one which had not been operated upon. A rubber tube led from the arm to a dial, on which a needle quivered and pulsated with clocklike regularity.

"This is a sphygmomanometer," announced the physician.

Gradually the movements of the pointer became fainter and fainter.

"Is he dead?" asked Endicott, in an awed voice.

"For the present," Quivven assured him.

Two workmen wheeled in a long narrow glass tank on a truck. At a signal from the nurse, they lifted the inert body and placed it in the tank. A piece of garden hose, ending in a spigot, hung from the ceiling. Turning on the spigot, the nurse filled the tank, until the body was submerged.

"Water-glass," explained Dr. Ronk. "In technical language, sodium silicate. What they preserve eggs in, you know."

The workmen wheeled out the tank.

"It now goes to the storehouse," continued Dr. Ronk, "until we need it again. It will keep indefinitely."

Endicott shuddered. "But how do you resuscitate one of those bodies?"

"Very simple," replied the doctor. "We take it out of its tank; we inject some heart-stimulant, a little fresh human blood, and

a hormone which stimulates both the propagation of red corpuscles in the marrow and the multiplying of the white corpuscles in the blood; and then we apply artificial respiration by
means of a pulmotor. The patient comes to life immediately,
but is very weak until his blood approaches normal. The recov-
ery, however, is always steady, although it takes several weeks,
and the patient has to be watched constantly for the first few
days, to guard against a relapse. We only lose about two per
cent."

Quivven and Eliot thanked him and withdrew. On their way
to the Administration Building, they stopped for a moment to
glance in through the door of a small building which Quivven
called the "schoolhouse." On rows of benches inside, there sat
or stood a queer mixture of animals: pigeons, rats, dogs of
various sizes and breeds, and a few other assorted varieties of
birds and beasts. The animals were intently watching a woman
who was writing on a blackboard at one end of the room.

"**WHAT'S** it all about?" asked Endicott in astonishment.

The golden Princess replied, "These animals have all been
operated upon, much as those humans whom you have just
seen. The insertion of the moth-grubs gives these beasts an
intelligence equal to ours, but of course no knowledge. However,
they can be taught to read and write in a very few months. We
teach them Porovian shorthand and English."

"But how can you get one of those large grubs into the tiny
brain of a rat or pigeon?"

"We can't, so we have perfected a special stunted variety of
moth for that purpose."

Then they continued on their way to the Administration
Building, where they entered the throne room. It was empty.
Quivven sat down on the scarlet throne, and motioned the
young man to a seat beside her.

"Eliot Endicott," said she in her alluring, exotic voice, placing
one hand confidingly on his arm, "do you now see why it is that
we are invincible? At several headquarters such as this our army

is growing steadily, night and day. Every Whoomang, from the lowliest to the highest, is of unquestioned and unquestionable loyalty to our cause, a loyalty that cannot be shaken or bought off. Can that be said of any *human* undertaking?"

Eliot shook his head, then asked, "But what is it all about— Quivven?"

"You ask that, do you, Eliot?" said she. "What of your investigation of our activities? I have read your report. It arrived here by the matter-transmitting apparatus, the morning after you did. It is very complete and thorough. I shudder to think what might have happened to us, if we hadn't captured you and stolen your report."

"Now you're making fun of me," said he, sheepishly.

"Indeed I'm not," she asserted. "It was a very good report— as far as it went. Did it not suggest to you what we are after?"

"Crime, bank-robberies, pay roll holdups, bootlegging, rum-running, loot, kidnaping. That doesn't sound like you, at all, Quivven!"

"Nor is it like me," the girl replied. "Crime is but a means to our end. Our object is empire! And when Boomalayla and Doggo and I divide the world between us, I want a man, a human man, to sit on the throne beside me—as you are sitting now, Eliot Endicott. Will you follow me to victory, and then be my prince-consort when the victory has been won?"

She lowered her voice and looked at him shyly, almost beseechingly. And hers was more than human beauty.

"Quivven, dear," exclaimed the enamored Endicott giddily, "I will follow you anywhere, and will sit at your feet until eternity."

"At my *side*, Eliot," said she, proudly.

"I will even become a Whoomang for your sake" he continued. Then suddenly a shadow of doubt passed across his face, and he said, "And yet—I won't be *me* any more, when they've given me a 'new-soul.' I may not be even human. Why, look, Quivven! Look at all these people in your organization! You and Aaron Cohen, and Dr. Chapin are the only ones who seem fully human. Swami Singh and Dr. Ronk are partly so. All the rest are mere animals, human machines, robots! You said, yourself, that I was the only interesting human being whom you had ever met. Have you ever met any human beings, Quivven? These around you are all denatured humans, automatons, Whoomangs with moth-grub souls!"

"You have given me food for thought," said the golden Princess levelly. "Cohen is not a Whoomang. He is without a newsoul, or still has his own soul, whichever you prefer to call it. That was a part of his compact when he brought us to this Earth. This leaves Dr. Chapin and myself as the only Whoomangs, out of thousands, who were not somehow stunted and blasted by the process. Will you trust me and follow me blindly, whichever way I decide?"

"I will trust you with my soul itself," promised the infatuated Endicott, throwing overboard all loyalty to the menaced nation whose respected official he had been.

QUIVVEN brightened. "Then, my consort, let me show you what it is to rule."

She pressed a button in the arm of the throne, and an obsequious lackey entered the room.

"Any reports?" she inquired regally.

"Yes, your majesty, the Speriden Company pay roll."

Presently there entered a rather alert-looking young male robot, who after making due obeisance, related a robbery of the night before.

The crime had really been absurdly simple. The organization had learned, through a member planted as an employee of the engineering force at the Speriden factory, that the vault in the main office-building had a mere wooden floor, although the ceiling and walls were brick. The pay roll money was always kept in a safe in this vault the night before pay day.

The planted employee knew the combination of the safe, but of course could not get into the vault, or even into the office building, at night. Armed watchmen, on their rounds, passed under and over and around the vault at frequent intervals. The vault door had a burglar alarm.

So, for weeks, Whoomang rats, with supremely intelligent moth-grub "new-souls," had gnawed a passageway, from a dark alley near by, through wall and floor, into a cupboard near the safe. This cupboard had a spring lock, and was one but seldom opened. Last night it had been left purposely ajar by the planted employee.

As soon as the vault was closed, at the five o'clock whistle, the rats, waiting in the cupboard, rushed out. They had a flash light with them. They rolled it out onto the floor, and pushed the button with their paws. A box had been placed near the safe for their convenience. Pushing it in place and mounting it, they quickly turned the knob. Long before morning, thirty thousand dollars was carted through the rat-hole in the wall to the alley, where at the last moment an automobile dashed in and picked it up. There was not a single clue to show where the money had gone. It might be months before any one would pull a drawer clear out of the cupboard and discover the gnawed hole, and even then no one would be likely to associate it with the robbery.

The story had a finishing touch of humor: the police detectives reported that it was undoubtedly "an inside job."

"Add that to your collection, my friend," said Quivven sweetly to Endicott, when the narrator had concluded. "Does not this throw considerable light on some of the cases which you have investigated? And now, Eliot, go to your room. I shall send for you presently. Meanwhile, never for one instant let go of the fact that you are mine."

She pressed his hand good-by, and he departed, to walk dazedly back to his quarters at the hospital.

The spell of the fragrant presence of Quivven the Golden-flame had lifted somewhat in the face of this familiar subject of pay roll robbery. He felt let down, oppressed. The full enormity of his guilt was just beginning to dawn upon him. He, Eliot Endicott, Assistant U.S. District Attorney, sworn to support the Constitution and laws of his country, had just pledged allegiance to an alien invader! And yet how sweet, how beautiful she was! His Quivven!

As soon as he was in his room, he stood in front of the dresser mirror, and held a hand-glass behind his head, in search of an excuse for his perfidy. But there was no scar, no shaved spot there. His soul was his own; he was still human, and hence fully responsible for his acts. He flung himself on his cot in bitter conflict with himself.

CHAPTER IX

INTRIGUES AMONG
THE WHOOMANGS

THE TRIUMVIRATE AND their premier, Aaron Cohen, were in deep conference in the throne room.

Cohen reported the capture and the mysterious escape of Lawrence Larrabee the evening before. But he announced that before going to bed, he had planted spies, both human and animal, in the village, and consequently felt confident that Larrabee could not make a single move without its becoming immediately known at headquarters.

"And now," said he, "let's play our trump card with Eliot Endicott. His sweetheart, Helyn Kent, is in our power. She has been given a new-soul. Dr. Chapin reports that the operation was successful, and that she is resting comfortably. She is one of us now. Let's take the young assistant district attorney to see her."

The eyes of Quivven the Goldenflame narrowed dangerously; then she smiled. "I myself can handle young Endicott," said she, "without any assistance from any other woman. He has already promised *me* to submit voluntarily to the operation."

"Well I'll be—" whistled Cohen, then checked himself, and finished instead with, "Your Majesty is certainly what we call a quick worker."

"Do you care for this prisoner?" inquired the huge antman, Doggo, through his radio speaker.

"What if I do?" countered Quivven swiftly.

"Remember, my dear, that you are a Whoomang."

"It is true that my soul is a Whoomang soul," said she, "and hence is utterly loyal to the cause; but my heart is the heart of a woman, and shall seek its mate where it will."

Doggo abruptly changed the subject.

"This Endicott person," said he; "you plan to turn him loose, do you, as soon as he is operated on? You plan to use him to confound the authorities, so as to keep them off our trail?"

"Why not?" asked Cohen.

"It seems to me," replied the antman, "that the authorities are already sufficiently confounded by his unexplained disappearance. If he goes back, he will have great difficulty in dissembling; in explaining why he does not reproduce his report from memory, for example. Let's keep him here."

"And let's turn the girl loose," suggested Quivven, "to prevent her father from coming after us, and so that she can spy on this newspaper reporter named Larrabee."

"And to keep her away from Eliot Endicott," added Doggo, a bit maliciously. Quivven scorned to reply to this.

DR. VICTOR CHAPIN was in his office in the hospital. At the particular moment when the knock sounded on his door, he was very much engrossed in kissing the pretty head nurse.

"Come in," said he, disengaging himself. "What is it?"

The door opened, and Quivven entered.

"I wish a word with you, alone," said she.

Chapin waved his hand with a gesture of dismissal, and the nurse withdrew.

"Now what can I do for your beautiful majesty?" he inquired.

Quivven dimpled, and then sobered.

"Will you do a personal favor for me?" she asked. "And tell no one, not even Doggo or the king?"

Chapin pursed up his lips reflectively.

"What will you give me, if I do?"

"Well—even a kiss or two," murmured Quivven provocatively.

He crushed Quivven the Goldenflame in his arms.

"A bargain!" he exclaimed. "Love is meat and drink to me. And a kiss from Quivven the Goldenflame would be nectar and ambrosia. I am at your service."

The princess drew closer, resting her shapely hand on his arm, and whispered, "I want you personally to operate on Eliot Endicott. And forget to put in a soul."

Dr. Chapin whistled softly, and stared long and appraisingly at the Goldenflame.

"I'm game, if you are," said he at last. Then he seized the girl passionately in his arms, and crushed her golden form to him.

Outside, in the corridor, the pretty nurse lifted from the keyhole a face white with jealous rage, and clenched her little hands in anger. She, too, had a woman's heart, in spite of her Whoomang soul.

Quivven blushingly disengaged herself, recovered somewhat her regal manner, and left the office despite the entreaties of the medical Lothario that she remain.

Shortly thereafter Aaron Cohen was announced by Chapin's secretary.

"Doctor," he inquired, "did you get a good view of that Kent girl?"

"No," replied Chapin. "One of my assistants operated. Why?"

"With all due respect to yourself as a Whoomang," said Cohen, "I hate to think of that beautiful girl as having been dehumanized. I thought that I was a cold intellectual, immune to women; but I could learn to love a girl like Helyn Kent. If I hadn't been so intent on getting that letter away from her, I might have noticed her beauty before; and her operation might have been prevented."

"But it was you who insisted on an immediate operation," interjected the young doctor, inwardly amused.

"Yes, I know, I know," admitted Cohen. "It was advisable, for the safety of the cause. I suppose it's too late to do anything now, but it's a pity, a great pity."

"Say, just what are you leading up to?" asked Chapin.

"Nothing, nothing," Cohen hastened to say; then with an attempt at sounding irrelevant: "If the soul were to be removed from a Whoomang, what would happen?"

"Nobody knows," replied the doctor, professionally. "It might restore to the person her own proper personality. It might leave her without any guiding intellect whatever, a driveling idiot. It might kill her. God knows. It's never been tried."

Cohen shuddered.

"Thank you," said he.

"Personally," asserted the doctor, "I prefer 'em as Whoomangs. Makes 'em more docile, you know."

"Chapin," exclaimed the other, "if I didn't respect you as a scientist and an ally, I should say that you were a perfect beast. Good day." And he stalked out.

THE DOCTOR, with a wry smile, went at once to Eliot Endicott's private ward.

"I want to have a confidential talk with you," he announced, closing and locking the door. After making sure there were no spying rats or pigeons about, he continued, "Her majesty Princess Quivven says that you are game to have a Whoomang soul implanted in your brain." Quivven had just been in to see her lover again, and her spell was again upon him.

"Yes," he admitted dully, "I—I suppose I am."

"Then let me tell you something in strictest confidence. I am to perform the operation in person, and I shall accidentally omit to put in the soul. You will retain your own personality, for Quivven the Goldenflame likes you just as you are, and does not dare risk a change."

Endicott's face lighted up with relief.

"How can I ever repay you, doctor?" he breathed.

"By pretending at every moment to be a Whoomang," Chapin replied solemnly. "Quivven's position, my position and even my life, are at stake if the king ever suspects. We are risking a great deal, Mr. Endicott."

"But how am I to be sure that the moth-grub was left out?"

Acting on a sudden impulse, Dr. Chapin made a confession, little guessing that the head nurse stood just outside the door, with her ear pressed against the panel. "I have no new-soul either, Mr. Endicott, although no one suspects it. I was one of the first humans on whom the newcomers operated. The Whoomangs were new to the conditions on this planet, they were hurried and clumsy; and somehow the moth-grub, picked out for me, failed to get put in. But I pretended to turn Whoomang, for the sake of my great future. You must do the same. Look around you. Is there a single person whom you have met in the organization, who has not been reduced to dumb bestiality by the operation? Cohen never underwent the process. Quivven? Yes; but she is not an ordinary human, she is a marvelous creature from another planet. The operation affects different species differently. Some it improves. Witness the king, the pigeons and the rats. Some it does not affect. Witness her majesty and Doggo. Some it debases. Witness every single one of our thousands of humans. If you ever breathe a word of your true condition, *that* will be your fate; a genuine operation."

So Eliot Endicott was operated on. But the outraged head nurse assisted in the operation.

CHAPTER X

TAKING THE OFFENSIVE

WHEN AARON COHEN'S runabout slewed almost into the ditch, Larry burst his bonds and jumped into the night. He landed sprawled out in the ditch, his cut bonds trailing behind him, his blindfold still clenched in one hand.

As he groped around in the darkness, he touched the open end of a large culvert. On sudden impulse, he crawled into this haven of refuge, dragging the ropes and the handkerchief with him, so as to leave no trace. Then he lay still, listening to the pursuit.

His late captors tramped up and down the ditch in vain, searching for him. The darkness and the weeds concealed the mouth of the drainpipe, and Cohen's searchlight did not happen to flash upon it.

Finally Larry heard Cohen exclaim, "If anything's happened to him, we can't afford to be seen here! Come on!"

He heard the sound of the departing car. Then he heard another car rumble by, on top of the culvert. After waiting what seemed a reasonable length of time, he started to crawl out; but the woods beside the road were lit by approaching headlights, and so he crawled rapidly back again into concealment. It was Cohen, and his two lumberjacks, returning.

There ensued another period of fruitless search, followed by the final departure of the pursuers. Larry waited a bit longer this time, then emerged from his hiding place, brushed himself off, and jog trotted back to town.

On the way, he did considerable thinking. That the men who had kidnaped him from his hotel room were part of the same outfit which had abducted the missing Federal attorney, seemed certain. That they knew that Larry was on their trail, seemed likely. But did they know that he was the same reporter whom they had shadowed as far as Rockingham Junction and there lost? And if so, how had they found it out? Perhaps that man, Jackson, from whom he had escaped in the taxi at the junction, had come on to Bartlett and had seen and recognized him. Little did he suspect the real truth of the tapping of Helyn Kent's subconscious mind by Swami Singh. He did not even know of Helyn's capture.

Did the criminals suspect that he had seen Eliot Endicott's letter to Helyn? That seemed preposterously unlikely. How could they even know of the existence of the letter? It certainly was lucky that he had followed his hunch, and had hidden the envelope, just before his capture and the rifling of his pockets.

At any event, there was nothing further that he could do that evening. Early in the morning he must get in touch with the Kents. In the meantime, he had better watch his step, for undoubtedly his late captors lay hidden in the vicinity of the Bartlett Hotel, awaiting his return.

For a moment, he thought of hunting up some other lodgings. But then he realized that every cent of his money had departed, when his pockets had been searched in the rumble seat of his captors' car. Thus he would have to return to his own hotel, where, in the absence of any baggage, he had already paid for a week's room and board in advance—or else sleep in the park, which might turn out to be too conspicuous. For spending money, he could wire the *Post* on the morrow.

On entering the town, Larry kept to the curb of the most brilliantly lighted sidewalks, carefully avoiding alley-mouths and dark doorways. Thus he reached the hotel in safety.

"Has any one phoned?" he inquired of the clerk.

"No," replied the desk clerk, Charley, "but here's a gentleman would like to see you."

Larry turned, half expecting to see Blackstone Kent standing there, but instead he confronted a total stranger, a portly individual with a broad-brimmed hat.

The reporter was instantly on the alert.

"I don't think that I've had the pleasure—" he began tentatively.

"Oh, that's the chief of police," explained Charley nonchalantly.

THE OFFICIAL, as if to corroborate this assertion, tilted back the edge of one lapel of his coat, exposing a silver star, and at the same time asked "Mr. O'Brien?"

That being the name under which Larry had registered.

"Yes, that's Mr. O'Brien," the clerk again butted in.

"Then would you mind stepping outside for a moment?" said the chief. "I want to have a few words with you."

When they reached the sidewalk, the official continued, "You are under arrest. Will you come peaceably, or shall I have to handcuff you?"

Larrabee's first impulse was to ask indignantly what in thunder they thought he had done. But then his agile mind leaped to a realization that this arrest was a veritable godsend, for it would insure him a good night's sleep in peace, absolutely free from all worry of his enemies disturbing him before morning.

So in his meekest tone, he replied, "I will come peaceably."

He could protest his innocence in the morning, and if he failed to convince the authorities, he could send for a lawyer. Why, he could even send for Blackstone Kent! What a capital scheme for getting in touch with Helyn's father!

So he walked along with the chief of police.

"Where have you been all evening?" asked the chief. "Remember; anything you say will be used against you."

"Then I'd better not say it," replied Larry, grinning. "I'll make a complete statement in the morning—in the presence of counsel."

The jail turned out not to be half bad, as jails go. The young reporter slept the sleep of the just, without a care in the world.

When he awoke the next morning, the sun was streaming through the bars. A pigeon was strutting up and down on the sill outside.

The boy smiled grimly.

"So they've located me already," he muttered to himself. "Everything that I say, with that bird present, certainly will be used against me."

He had just completed dressing, when the chief of police appeared at the door of the cell.

"How are you feeling this morning?" the official inquired.

"Never felt better in my life," replied Larry truthfully.

"All ready for your confession?"

"Nothing doing, chief, until I get a lawyer."

"Have you any particular lawyer in mind? Now I know a real capable young fellow, who will defend you dirt cheap."

Larry glanced at the pigeon, which had ceased its strutting, and was standing motionless on the window sill, with its head cocked on one side.

"Let's talk in your office, chief," he suggested.

The office had no outside window. As they entered it, and sat down, Larry noticed this fact and heaved a sigh of relief.

"And now may I ask," said he, "just what I've been arrested for?"

"As a suspicious character."

"Fair enough," admitted the reporter. "I *am* a suspicious character. Very suspicious. But it's not you whom I suspect; so why arrest me?"

"It's *you* that's suspected," snorted the humorless official.

"What of? Or rather, of what?" asked Larry.

"Search me!" replied the chief. "Don't you know what you've done?"

"My conscience is as clear as a newborn babe's," asserted the prisoner. "But before I submit to any more of this third degree stuff," and he smiled grimly at the memory of some real third degree sessions he had known about. "I should like a lawyer. Would you mind sending for Blackstone Kent?"

The chief's jaw dropped.

"What?" he exclaimed. "Say that again."

"I said," repeated Larry, "would you mind sending for Blackstone Kent? What's the matter with him? Isn't he a good lawyer?"

"Well, I reckon!" exclaimed the still surprised official. "He's the best criminal lawyer in all New England. But don't you realize? It's he who had you arrested!"

It was now Larry's turn to be astounded.

"Well, I'll be hanged!" said he. "What for?"

Just then the telephone rang. The chief picked up the receiver. Whoever was at the other end of the line was talking loudly enough for Larry to hear.

"Is this the police station?"

"Yes."

"Blackstone Kent speaking. Have you a man named Larrabee there? Charley over at the hotel says you arrested him last night."

"No such thing," began the chief.

But Larry hastily interposed, "I'm Larrabee.

That's my real name."

"Just a minute, Mr. Kent, there's a prisoner here who says that his name's Larrabee."

"Then I'll be right over."

The policeman wiped his brow, and stared at his prisoner in justified perplexity.

A FEW minutes later Blackstone Kent bustled in.

"Mr. Larrabee," said he, holding out his hand, "a thousand pardons. I just found your note. Why didn't you give it to me in person, instead of merely leaving it on my doorstep?"

"I did," replied the reporter, with a wry mouth, "but you threw it in my face, and slammed the door."

"Again, I say, a thousand pardons," apologized the lawyer. "And then, to add injury to insult, I had you arrested, thinking that you might be able to throw some light on my daughter's disappearance."

"Helyn disappeared!" exclaimed Larry.

"You seem quite familiar with my daughter, for one who has never met her," remarked Kent, with a tired ghost of a smile. "Yes, Helyn failed to come home last night." His voice shook with emotion as he said this, but he steadied himself and went on:

"She is not with any of our friends, and no trace has been found of her, or of the beach wagon which she was driving. The police of all the surrounding towns have been notified, but none of them have seen either her or the car. Your note suggests that you may be able to help me."

"I believe that I can," replied the reporter soberly, "but, if the chief will pardon me, what I have to say is for your ears alone."

The official promptly and obligingly excused himself, but Kent waved him back into his seat.

"No need to drive you out of your own office," said he, "We can talk over at the hotel."

As Kent and Larry left the jail, the former whispered, "He might have the place wired with a dictaphone, you know. He seemed too darned obliging."

Nothing more was said on the subject, until they reached the hotel. Up to room 31 they went. There was a pigeon on the sill. Larry shooed it away, and slammed down the window. Then he began the narration of what he knew of the disappearance of Eliot Endicott, of the pterodactyl which he had seen flying through the night, of the theft of Endicott's report, of the pigeons in his editor's window, and of the trip to Rockingham Junction and beyond. He even admitted the sudden interest which he had felt for the beautiful girl, Kent's daughter, on the train.

Just as he was about to tell the episode of the letter in the post office, he noticed a rat, standing silent and intent in a corner.

"Another spy!" he exclaimed and hurled a book at it.

It scampered down a hole, and Larry promptly stuffed the hole with newspaper. Then he continued his story, in a much lower tone of voice. Also he produced the envelope from under the dresser-top towel, and showed it to his visitor.

When he had reached the point where he had tramped out to Bemises, and had made his fruitless attempt to see Helyn, her father interrupted with an account of the call which he had received from the proprietor of the Jones Lumber Camp.

Then Larry in turn interrupted to ask, "What kind of car did he have?"

Blackstone Kent described it.

Whereupon Larry said grimly, "I took a little ride in that same car later in the evening."

And then recounted the story of his own kidnaping and escape.

When the two men had finished comparing notes, they were both convinced of certain basic facts, namely: that the hand of super-criminals on whose trail Assistant District Attorney Endicott had been working, had kidnaped him; that the Jones Lumber Camp was an important cog in their organization; that the missing Eliot Endicott was probably at that camp; that "Mr. Jones" himself was one of the men who had tried to kidnap Larry; and that Helyn was probably in the clutches of these same criminals, perhaps because Eliot Endicott had been forced to admit sending her his S.O.S. letter.

What they couldn't understand was how that letter had come to be readdressed to the Jones Lumber Camp. They puzzled quite a lot over this, though they admitted that it really was a relatively immaterial detail.

THEY decided upon their plan of action. Each was to be always armed. Kent was immediately to phone all the surrounding towns for possible word of Helyn, while Larry called up the Boston *Post* to ascertain if there were any further clues as to the missing assistant district attorney, and to tip off the paper to the description of the Boston headquarters of the criminals, as stated in the missing man's letter to his cousin Helyn.

Then they were to meet again in Larry's room, and drive out to Morton's together.

Larry's phone call to the *Post* developed the fact that the authorities had uncovered no more clues, or at least had not divulged any. A reporter was at once detailed to try and find the office building described in Eliot Endicott's letter.

As Larry stepped out of the booth, he saw a familiar face—a young man of about his own age.

"Jack Blakeslee!" he exclaimed. "What are you doing up in this neck of the woods?"

"Flying," replied his friend. "My plane's over in a field just outside of town. And you?"

"Oh, I'm just on a vacation," lied Larry.

"More likely on a story of some sort," opined his friend. "But if you're really on a vacation, come along with me. I've got an extra seat."

"That gives me an idea!" exclaimed the reporter. "Come up to my room."

"I'll be up in just a minute. What's the number?"

"Thirty-one."

"O.K., then."

Larry went up to his room alone. The air was stuffy and oppressive, so he flung open the window again. There on the sill was the inevitable pigeon.

Exasperated, he heaved a tumbler at it. The missile struck

the bird squarely. Rushing to the window, Larry looked out on the shed roof just below, the pigeon was flapping feebly. Then it lay still. Impelled by a sudden impulse, Larry climbed out onto the roof, and retrieved the dead body.

Back in his room, he turned the inert form over in his hands, idly examining it. It seemed to be an ordinary enough pigeon, except in one particular. There was a noticeable scar on the back of its head.

"Maybe they pumped some brains into it," he snickered skeptically.

Then his attention was distracted by the flapping of wings outside. Hastily throwing the body into a bureau drawer, and slamming the drawer shut, he turned just in time to see another pigeon settle upon the window sill.

"This is too much!" he exclaimed, so he hastened down stairs and sought the clerk.

To him the reporter complained of his room being overrun with rats and pigeons, and demanded that something be done about it. Then Jack Blakeslee reappeared, and the two went up to room 31 together.

The paper was out of the rat hole, from which the tip of the rodent's nose now shyly protruded, and there were two pigeons and a sparrow on the window sill. But just as Larry was looking around for something more to heave, a large, sleek, well-fed black cat sauntered into the room from the hall.

"Now that's what I call service!" exclaimed Larry. "I just complained of vermin to the clerk, and here he's sent up the hotel cat, to keep them away from me."

The cat rubbed against his leg and purred. He reached down and scratched the side of its head. Then it jumped up onto the window sill, where it sat gazing dreamily off into space. The pigeons, and the sparrow, and the rat had departed.

"Now we can talk," said the boy, "while kitty stays on guard, to keep off eavesdroppers."

"Eavesdroppers?" asked Blakeslee, perplexed. "How can a cat keep off eavesdroppers?"

"Just listen to my story," replied Larry, and you will understand."

Briefly he sketched to his friend all the momentous events which had occurred. Blackstone Kent arrived, was introduced, and reported that there was still no word of Helyn. Then Lawrence Larrabee broached his plan.

"It will do no good," said he, "for us to get out a search warrant, and go through the lumber camp, for this would give them sufficient time to spirit away both Eliot Endicott and Miss Kent. So let's fly over the camp in Jack's plane, and spy on them by surprise."

Blackstone Kent expressed immediate approval of the plan; then produced two automatic pistols, which he had just purchased for himself and Larry, and handed one to each of the men.

"Start at once," said he. "There is no time to be lost."

"Suits me," exclaimed Jack Blakeslee.

So Larry collected his few belongings, and they departed.

ON THEIR way out of the hotel, Larry stopped to thank the clerk for the loan of the cat.

"Cat?" asked Charley. "What sort of a cat?"

So the reporter described it.

"No," said the clerk, "we haven't any cat in this here hotel. And what's more I don't know any one in town as has a black one. May belong to some summer folks though. Let's take a look at it."

So together they went up to the room, but the black cat was nowhere to be seen. What did it matter, anyway? The cat, no matter whose it was, had served its purpose by enabling them to make their plans in privacy, not spied on by pigeons or rats.

Blackstone Kent drove them out to Jack's plane, and soon the two were soaring away. The lumber camp was easily located, lying to the southward toward Mt. Chocorua. As soon as they identified it, they circled away, descended to a lower level, and then swept back again just above the treetops.

"Why, this is a regular military camp!" exclaimed Larry. "Look at the barbed wire fence all around it! Look at the armed guards patrolling the fence!"

"And look at what's going on in that tower!" Jack shouted back. "They evidently expect us."

In the midst of the camp there stood a high wooden observation tower, like those used by fire wardens, quite an expected thing to find in a lumber camp. But on its platform, there stood two men operating what looked like a searchlight, which they were turning frantically toward the oncoming plane.

"Why a searchlight in the daytime?" Larry exclaimed.

And then, as if in answer to his query, the motor sputtered and stopped completely.

Blakeslee tried to reach a point beyond the boundaries of the camp, before crashing, but he was flying too low. When he saw that he wasn't going to make it, the young aviator changed his tactics, and side-slipped down into a small clearing between the trees.

"Run for it!" he shouted, as the two of them clambered out of the plane.

Already a band of about a dozen lumberjacks were charging toward them through the woods.

So the two youths ran. Fleet of foot, they were beginning to outdistance their heavier pursuers, when the high barbed wire fence loomed ahead.

To make matters worse, a burly guard stood between them and the fence, with a drawn automatic in his hand.

CHAPTER XI

THE IGNITION RAY

JACK AND LARRY were armed. When they found their escape blocked by the guard who stood with drawn gun at the barbed wire fence, Jack Blakeslee drew his own automatic and fired quickly. As a reserve officer of the air corps, he had not only learned flying, he had also had considerable practice on the target range, and this now stood him in very good stead.

His shot struck just where he had aimed it, the guard's forearm, and the fellow's weapon clattered to the ground. The guard, surprised and momentarily stunned by the wound, staggered backward and clutched the fence for support with his wounded left hand. For the present, he was disposed of, but the dozen lumberjacks were rapidly nearing, and the high woven fence, topped with its three strands of barbed wire, appeared to present just as insuperable an obstacle as before.

Frantically the two men looked around them for some way of escape.

To one side of the guard there was a gate in the fence. It was evidently unfastened, for an open padlock on a chain dangled beside it. Probably that is why this particular sentinel had been stationed here.

With a shout of joy and triumph, the two fugitives rushed forward. But even as they did so, a siren whistle sounded in the camp behind them. The guard, who was still clinging to the fence, let out a gurgling scream, slumped to the ground, with his hand still clutching the wires, and began a ghastly twitching dance, while the cords knotted in his neck, his face turned purple, his eyes rolled in their sockets, and guttural noises issued from his mouth.

"Back! Back!" shouted Larry, recoiling in horror at the sight. "The fence is electrified!"

The poor wounded guard had been unable in time to heed the siren warning, and thus unwittingly had sacrificed his life to warn Jack and Larry from the fate intended for them.

Now the lumberjacks were almost upon them.

Seizing a piece of broken tree-branch that lay on the ground near by, Larry pushed it against the gate to slide it to one side. By this time the whole fence was humming with the high-tension current. A nauseating smell of burned flesh was wafted toward them from the dead body of the guard. Sparks snapped at the end of the branch, as Larry touched it to the gate, and his arms tingled and twitched.

But he persisted, in spite of the pain, and got the gate open, just as their pursuers reached them.

Risking death if they so much as brushed against a wire, the two crowded through the opening. The lumberjacks halted abruptly, not daring to approach the death-dealing electricity. The two spies were safely through, and running off into the woods.

But one of the lumberjacks picked up a sizable stone, and hurled it with unerring accuracy after the rapidly departing pair. It grazed the side of Larry's head and he went down. Then the siren sounded twice, and the twelve men, as though released from a spell, charged through the opening.

Jack pulled Larry to his feet, thrust one arm around his waist, and backed away from their pursuers, firing as he went. He was mad enough now to shoot to kill, but he was hampered by the inert body of his friend. Even so, one of the lumberjacks pitched forward onto his face, and the others halted.

Then, *crack!* And a bullet pinged past them.

Some one was shooting at them with a rifle from the watch-tower. Jack promptly dragged Larry behind some trees, inserted another clip in his automatic, and stood at bay.

Larry's eyes opened and he stumbled to his feet. Jack seized his friend's hand, and dragged him off through the woods. Gradually Larry recovered, as they ran. Soon he seemed his old self again.

"They'll be after us," he opined. "They'll expect us to make straight for Bartlett. Bartlett lies northwest from here; so let's head due north, and strike the road to Morton's."

THE TWO friends settled down to a fast walk. No sounds of pursuit were heard. Quite evidently they had eluded their enemies. They said nothing as they strode along, for they were saving their breath for walking.

Soon they found a north-bound trail, which facilitated travel.

After about twenty minutes, Larry suddenly stopped and laid his hand on Jack's arm, saying, "Listen!"

They listened. From behind them, faint but unmistakable, came the deep baying of dogs.

"Bloodhounds!" exclaimed Larry. "Bloodhounds, probably with human minds! Run if you never did before!"

And the two of them began to run again.

The path finally became rough and bumpy.

"Feels like railroad ties," panted Jack.

"It is!" replied Larry. "Look."

In front of them in a slight clearing, the ground made an abrupt dip and rise again, and directly ahead a wooden bridge with two iron rails spanned the little ravine. They had been running along the track of an abandoned logging railroad, which was so overgrown with moss and grass that they hadn't recognized it for what it was.

Out onto the bridge they trotted, when with a ripping crash the ties gave way beneath them. They grabbed for the rails which still hung aloft. Somehow they both slid unhurt to the ground, which was not more than ten feet beneath. Then they ran across the valley, up the farther bank, and onto the track once more.

The baying of the hounds came nearer and nearer behind them. At last the fleeing pair reached a gorge, through which rushed a mountain torrent. The sides were precipitous stone cliffs. The railroad track ended abruptly at the edge. On the rocks below there were a few twisted pieces of rail and some broken timbers.

The fugitives paused for breath at the edge. The baying behind them changed to a series of short sharp yelps.

Jack exulted, "The pack has lost the trail where we fell through that bridge. It'll be several minutes before they find it again."

"No it won't," panted Larry. "Their human minds will lead them right to the spot where we landed."

And he was right, for even as he was speaking, the full-throated baying commenced again. "Then let's fool their minds, in a way that wouldn't fool a real dog," suggested Blakeslee.

"Let's cross this stream, and *not* hit the railroad again on the other side."

"Let's not even cross," added Larry. "This river runs under the Morton road, so we can stay on this side, and still get to Morton's."

Quickly they clambered down the face of the cliff into the swirling water below, floundered along with the current for some distance, and then laboriously scaled the cliff again at a point on the same side about a hundred yards downstream from where they had entered the water.

The pack of hounds was rapidly coming down the old railroad. The two lay concealed in a thicket, watching tensely.

Presently four huge bloodhounds appeared at the edge of the ravine. The dogs didn't even hesitate. Scrambling down the face of the cliff, they obliquely forded the stream, landing just about opposite the hiding place of the two boys.

The dogs had considerable difficulty in getting up the other cliff, but at last they made it, and in full cry as though actually on the trail again, they dashed upstream along the cliff-top.

The two fugitives melted into the woods, and rapidly made their way downstream, on the opposite bank from their Whoomang bloodhound pursuers.

An excited yelping behind them indicated that the bloodhounds had reached the continuation of the railroad track, and had found no scent of their quarry. Jack and Larry chuckled, as they ran on.

The yelping ceased, and an ominous silence ensued.

"I don't like that," remarked Larry. "They're up to something."

"They're letting their dog-sense work now," replied Jack. "Now we're in for trouble."

EVEN as he spoke, one deep-throated bay broke from the woods behind them, followed by yelpings at several widely separated points.

"Run!" exclaimed Larry. "Our only hope now is to reach Morton's ahead of them."

The two fugitives dodged through the trees as fast as they could. But there was no path here; the low-running hounds had the advantage, and rapidly gained on them.

The pair reached a thick wall of brush. Frantically pushing their way through it, they emerged upon a road!

Coming down the road toward them from their left was a touring car. Jumping into the middle of the road, they held up their right hands as a signal for the car to stop; but the driver merely honked his horn, and did not diminish his speed. The dogs were nearly upon them.

The two men, as though impelled by a single thought, whipped out their guns, and leveled them at the oncoming car. Larry fired, and his bullet shattered the windshield. The car came to a grinding stop.

"Quick! Give us a lift!" shouted Larry.

The man obligingly opened the door; but as Larry clambered

in, he felt something hard and cylindrical pressed against his ribs, and a voice barked in his ear, "One word, and I'll drill you! Now hand over that gat!"

Larry handed it over.

Jack meanwhile, counting on his friend to attend to the man in the car, had wheeled around with his back to them, and was intently watching the edge of the road, with weapon raised.

At that instant a hound's head, and two clawing forepaws, made their appearance through the thicket. *Crack!* went Jack's pistol, and the dog pitched forward into the ditch, to twitch there convulsively for a few moments, and then lie still.

With a pleased smile, Jack turned around. Then his face fell, for he was looking into the muzzle of the automatic of the driver of the car.

But, as the driver pointed his gun at Jack, this left Jack's partner uncovered. Instantly, Larry leaped upon the man and seized his gun-arm.

Jack swung up his own automatic and shouted, "I've got the drop on *you,* now!"

The driver of the car subsided.

But, at that instant three dogs clawed their way through the bushes. Jack gained the car with one jump. Then the blood-hounds were upon them.

Larry wrenched the gun from the man's hand, and buried its muzzle in the man's neck.

"Start the car!" he commanded.

The man obeyed. As the automobile started, the three dogs made a frantic attempt to scramble over the side of the car, and get at the three men.

Larry shifted his gun to his left hand, and caught one of the brutes a blow on the snout with his right fist, spilling it off into the road. Jack shot one of the others through the head. The third dog jumped off, and went sliding into the ditch, from which it picked itself up and joined its sole surviving companion.

As the car sped up, and rounded a turn the two bloodhounds could be seen standing at the top of a rise, gazing after the departing men.

A little farther on, the motor began to sputter and miss, and finally died altogether. The car coasted to a stop.

"What's the matter?" snapped Jack.

"Search me," replied the driver, unconcernedly.

"You're faking!" Larry charged menacingly.

The two dogs came in sight, loping down the road behind them, but stopped just out of range of their guns.

"Get this car going!" exclaimed Larry, exasperated. "We've got to escape from those damned bloodhounds."

The man looked back.

"Say, what is this, anyhow?" he asked. "Uncle Tom's Cabin? Or are you runaway convicts?"

"Neither!" snapped Jack. "But you'd better get us to Morton's in a hurry if you know what's good for you."

"Say!" exclaimed the man. "You aren't planning to hold up Blackstone Kent, are you?"

"I should say not!" replied Larry, in a tone that carried conviction. "He's a friend of ours! We're hurrying there for protection!"

"Then why didn't you say so before?" exclaimed the man. "I'm Kent's chauffeur. Let's go."

Whereupon he started up the supposedly stalled car, and soon they were on their way, again, with the two hounds loping behind, just out of range.

THE MAN actually was Blackstone Kent's chauffeur. On their arrival at Morton's, Kent listened with intent interest to their adventures.

"I guess there can be no doubt now," he commented, when they had finished, "as to the caliber of the criminals with whom we are dealing."

"You know," confessed Jack Blakeslee, "I must admit that I

thought at first that Larrabee's story was all a hop-dream, so I went into the thing just for the fun of it. But my doubts were knocked out of me, pretty soon after we crashed. Say, you should have seen those hell-hounds! They were positively human!"

"What about Helyn?" interrupted Larry, suddenly, remembering.

Blackstone Kent's face sobered.

"I haven't heard any news of her yet," said he.

"Then it's me for Bretton Woods!" exclaimed Blakeslee.

"What for?" asked Larry.

"To get another plane."

But Blackstone Kent sadly shook his head.

"It's no use," said he. "I've figured out what that searchlight thing must be. It stopped your motor. It must be the same as the ignition-interfering ray, which the French Army were reported as having perfected several years ago. A band of criminals, who can transmit persons through space by wireless in the way that Eliot Endicott's letter mentioned, and who can put human intelligence into pigeons and bloodhounds, may very likely he able to stall an airplane motor."

Blakeslee, however, instead of appearing downcast at this pronouncement, actually brightened up.

"Jove! I have it!" he exclaimed. "I'll borrow Carson's plane."

"One plane would be as bad as another," Kent lugubriously admitted.

"Not Carson's," replied the young aviator "for his is a Packard."

"What difference does that make?"

The airman surveyed the older man with a look of tolerant amusement.

"A Packard," said he, "has a Diesel engine."

"Well?"

"Don't you understand? A Diesel engine has no ignition, so this ray can't bother it!"

"Yea!" exclaimed Larry, jumping to his feet. "Let's go!"

Kent's face suffused with interest and hope.

"My man will drive you right over to Bretton Woods," said he warmly.

It was late in the afternoon when the two men reached Bretton Woods. Carson was still there, and Blakeslee readily obtained the loan of his plane for the morrow. Blakeslee and Larrabee then spent the evening fraternizing with the aviators and attendants of the Mount Washington flying field, but never a word did the two adventurers breathe of what had happened that day, or of what they suspected was ahead of them.

They spent the night at one of the hotels. For two days it rained, and they fretted and fumed and killed time. They phoned frequently to Mr. Kent, but he still had received no clue as to Helyn's whereabouts. During the third night of their stay at Bretton Woods, the weather cleared.

Bright and early the next morning, Carson took them out to the field and gave Blakeslee a short trial flight in the Diesel-motored plane. Then they came down; Carson surrendered his seat to Larrabee, and Jack and Larry soared up and away to the eastward.

As they took off, Larry said dubiously, "I hope that you're right about that ray not being able to stall a Diesel engine, for if it can, we are sure out of luck!"

IT WAS not long before they sighted the Jones Lumber Camp ahead of them. But what a different scene from that of their last visit!

As they came into view, all was activity. Men ran to lock all the fence gates. Quite a number of others climbed to the top of the watch-tower. A crowd gathered in front of one of the buildings!

Then the siren sounded a single blast, and the men sprang away from the boundary fence. The pseudo-searchlight on the tower-top trained its invisible beam on the oncoming plane. By the side of the searchlight, there stood two men with machine guns.

"We're in for a hot reception," remarked Jack. "They are evidently expecting us. If we crash inside the fence, it's good night for us! And look at the audience that's come out to witness our finish!"

Pulling his joy-stick quickly backward as he approached the camp, he rose at a sharp angle. The searchlight was now turned full upon them, and yet their motor never missed a beat.

"Good old Diesel!" exclaimed Jack. "And will you look at the masquerade!"

In the midst of the "audience" there were a huge slate-gray winged dragon, a black ant as large as a horse, and a golden female statue swathed in clinging robes of blue. Close beside the statue stood a young man. All the others of the crowd were at a respectful distance from these four. And then the statue moved, and appeared to be speaking to the young man beside it.

"Why, she's alive!" shouted Larry.

At just this moment, one of the machine guns on the tower-top cut loose at the oncoming plane. A gash of red appeared on the side of Jack's head, and the plane, relieved of his guidance, suddenly plunged forward and down, straight at the tower.

It was amusing to see the rapidity and consternation with which the occupants of the tower dropped searchlight and both machine guns, and flattened themselves upon the platform. One of the men even dived off into space, and striking the ground below, remained crumpled and motionless where he landed.

But Larry was in no mood for humor. Although he knew nothing of flying, he seized the auxiliary stick and yanked it backward; and the plane, responding, just barely cleared the tower.

Jack dazedly sat up, wiped the blood out of his eyes with the back of one hand, and looked around. Then, realizing the situation, he grasped the control-stick, and leveled the ship.

Circling, he headed back for the camp once more. But the

men on the tower had had enough, and were rapidly descending its spiral staircase, in spite of the angry shouts of a man on the ground. The dragon, the antman, and the golden girl and her male companion had disappeared.

The two men flew over the camp as low as the trees would permit, studying all possible details, but no one offered them any further violence. The morale of the enemy appeared to have been thoroughly wrecked.

Several times the flyers circled round and round across the camp, and then when they had satisfied themselves that they had seen all that was visible, they headed for Bretton Woods.

Jack's head was bleeding pretty freely, but he insisted that it was only a scratch.

CHAPTER XII

IN LEAGUE WITH THE ENEMY

AT BRETTON WOODS, they turned the plane back to Carson, adjured him to keep his mouth shut about Jack's wound, and hurried to Kent's car.

"Wasn't that golden girl a prize bathing beauty?" Jack exclaimed as they drove away from the landing-field.

"Yes," assented his friend. "But did you notice who was with her?"

"Who?"

"The missing Eliot Endicott!"

"Did you see any sign of the Kent girl?"

"Not a trace," replied Larry sadly, and lapsed into silence.

Blackstone Kent was awaiting them in the driveway at Morton's.

"We've found Eliot Endicott!" they shouted, as they drove up.

But their host's face registered no joy.

"Helyn has been found," he said dully.

"Alive?" said the two in unison.

"Yes," said Blackstone Kent.

Then why the gloom? Sobered and puzzled, they got out of the car.

"She's upstairs asleep now," Blackstone Kent continued. "She seems to be a little out of her mind. The police found her wandering dazedly in the fields about thirty miles from here. She knows who she is; but not very much more. And she has abso-lutely no recollection where she has been or what she has been doing the past four days."

Larrabee and Blakeslee were too shocked and horrified to make any comment, but went inside, where Jack's wound was dressed.

Helyn came down from her nap, much rested, and appar-ently perfectly well. Her father was greatly relieved. True, she could remember nothing which had happened from the time she had entered the post office four days ago to the morning of the present day. But apart from this bit of amnesia, her mind now appeared perfectly clear. The three men decided that it would do no harm to approach her gently on the subject of Eliot Endicott's letter. In fact, to mention to her the letter might result in restoring her memory of the intervening events.

So the two visitors were introduced to the girl. Larry then, with his best Irish ingratiatory manner, told the girl how he had frantically tried to find out who she was on the train, how he had gone beyond his station in order to get off with her at Bartlett, and how he had mooned around Bartlett all one day in the hope of catching a glimpse of her.

Through all the narration, she watched him with an amused, but slightly embarrassed smile. But when he mentioned seeing her open a letter in the post office, she became visibly agitated.

"I remember getting the letter," said she; "but not its contents. I don't remember anything further.

There must have been some terrible news in that letter. Maybe that's what's the matter with me."

"Can't you recollect a single bit of the contents?" urged her father. "Think. Think hard!"

But the girl shook her head sadly, positively.

At a sign from Blackstone Kent, Larry at once cut in with, "The letter was from your cousin, Eliot Endicott."

"How do you know?" exclaimed Helyn, wheeling and facing him. Then steadying herself with an effort, she said dully, "But it couldn't have been. Eliot has disappeared. Probably he has been killed. He couldn't write anybody a letter."

"Miss Kent," persisted Larry, "I read that letter over your shoulder in the post office. I read every word of it."

But she shook her head, with narrowed eyes. Said she, "Don't think me rude, but I don't believe it. You can't prove it."

Then she bit her lip, as though she wished she had not spoken in just that way.

"Miss Kent," said Larry, "I have the envelope of that letter. Your cousin's handwriting can be easily identified."

"What!" she gasped. "Where is it?"

Larry felt in several of his pockets. Then his face fell.

"It's still under the towel on top of the dresser in the Bartlett hotel," said he.

"We must get it at once!" exclaimed Kent.

"Come on, I'll drive you down. Mr. Blakeslee, you stay with Helyn."

"He needn't bother," said the girl, listlessly. "I feel tired, with all this excitement. I think I'll lie down again."

Kissing her father dutifully, she dragged herself upstairs.

"Watch her, Blakeslee," whispered Kent. "Come on, Larrabee."

SOON they were speeding to town in Kent's car.

"Do you know, Larrabee," asserted Kent, when they were well on their way, "Helyn was lying to us."

"What makes you think so?" demanded Larry in surprise.

"I'm a lawyer," the older man explained, "and I have had a lifetime of experience in studying the behavior of witnesses on the stand. I can tell almost infallibly, from the manner of a witness, whether or not he is telling the truth; and I am sure that Helyn was lying. Oh, Mr. Larrabee, it's terrible! My little girl never lied to me before! Why did she? What is the matter with her?"

They drove the rest of the way to Bartlett in silence, each immersed in gloomy thoughts.

At the hotel, they ascertained from the clerk that Room 31 had not been occupied since Larry's departure, so they obtained the key, and hurried up. But the envelope was not under the towel on the top of the dresser. The towel was the same old towel, all right, for Larry recognized a peculiarly shaped hole in one corner, which had attracted his attention before. But the letter was gone. Kent asked the clerk to send for the chambermaid, but she denied having taken any envelope. In fact, she hadn't even emptied the wastebasket since Mr. Larrabee was there.

As a last resort, they started hunting through the drawers; and when they opened a certain one of those in the bureau, out flew a small brown moth, accompanied by a rather putrid smell. The moth flew straight through the open crack of the window, and disappeared. The rank smell proved to emanate from the dead body of a pigeon lying in the drawer.

It was the spying pigeon which Larry had killed by throwing a tumbler at it, and whose body he had then examined, and thrust into the drawer, and promptly forgotten. Now he fished it out gingerly, and showed it to Kent, pointing to the strange scar which he had noticed before on the back of its head.

But now, in place of the scar, there was a round open hole. The two men discussed this phenomenon, but they could make nothing out of it, and so they resumed their search for the envelope. But it was nowhere to be found.

"The Jones Lumber Camp crowd have undoubtedly got it," opined Larrabee, "but when and how?"

On their way back to Morton's, the conversation finally shifted to the pigeon again.

"As a lawyer," announced Kent, "I never let go of any bit of evidence, no matter how irrelevant it may seem, and so I can't help feeling that the opening of that scar in the pigeon's head had some bearing on the mystery of the uncanny mentality of the bird. Have you noticed any similar scar or hole in any other animal recently?"

Larry's face suddenly lighted up with a forgotten recollection.

"The cat!" he exclaimed. "The black cat which nobody owned, and which sat in my room while I was talking to Jack Blakeslee. I can't swear that it had such a scar, but I remember now that there was a small spot on the back of its head where the fur looked a bit ragged. Why, perhaps the cat was a spy, too! That would account for the fact that the Jones outfit was expecting us when we flew over their lumber camp the first time."

"Then we must keep our eyes peeled for animals with scars," said Kent.

BACK at Morton's once more, Blakeslee met them at the gate; and he was visibly agitated.

"I'm going to talk to you right here, out in the open, where no one can possibly overhear us," he said. "Are there any animals within earshot?"

All three men glanced carefully around them, but saw none. Then Jack continued, "Of course, you didn't get the envelope.'

"You know where it is?" asked Larry eagerly, but his friend shook his head.

"No," said he, "but listen till I tell you what happened here after you two left. It suddenly occurred to me that, as the enemy always seem to know our plans as fast as we make them, they might easily beat you to the hotel. So I rushed to the phone, to call up the hotel clerk, and ask him to get the envelope and hold it until you reached there. But Miss Helyn was already on the line, on an extension set upstairs, I guess."

Kent started. Then nodded.

Blakeslee continued, "As I cut in, she was just saying, 'Aaron, dear, get some one to the hotel quick. The envelope of the Eliot Endicott letter is under the towel on the top of the dresser in Room 31. Father and Larrabee are on the way there for it right now. Hurry!' Then a man's voice said, 'Yes, dear. Thanks.' That was all. They both hung up, and I naturally tried all the more frantically to phone the hotel. But I couldn't even raise central. The line seemed to have gone dead."

"Cut, undoubtedly," remarked Kent grimly. "Let's see."

But central promptly answered, "Numbah, plee-uz."

So whatever had been the matter with the line had been purely temporary.

"Who is this Aaron person?" asked Larry. "That ought to give us a clue."

"So far as I am aware," Kent replied sadly, "my daughter knows no one of that name."

It was easy to see that he was deeply shocked by the proof of his daughter's perfidy.

They went inside. Helyn greeted them almost gayly.

"Did you bring the envelope?" she asked, impishly.

"No," admitted Larry.

"I rather thought there wasn't any such letter," she asserted, with a smile.

None of the three men cared to press the point.

After supper, Larry took Helyn for a walk. She played up to him in her prettiest manner. The night was glamorous. The girl was so solicitously interested in his recent adventures, that he found it difficult to withhold any information. He did not want to be rude, and yet he strove constantly to remember that she was in some way, and for some unknown reason, linked with the enemy.

It hardly seemed possible. Was he not letting his imagination get away with itself?

He cudgelled his mind for some plausible explanation of her behavior. Almost he succeeded in persuading himself that she was merely playing a joke; that this "Aaron" person was merely some friend of hers; and that she had sent him to steal the envelope, just so that she could say "I told you so." But then there came to the reporter a realization that this explanation, although exonerating to her morality, was positively damning to her mentality, for no girl in her right mind would joke about so serious a matter as the kidnapping of her cousin.

Jealousy prompted Larry to demand of her who this man "Aaron" was, and what he meant in her life, but he wisely stayed his tongue.

But, all in all, the walk was a very pleasant one for him, and his companion didn't succeed in pumping much information out of him. When they returned to the house, however, Larry felt suddenly let down, dissatisfied. Helyn had been just a little too forward, too easy, unlike the girl on the train as he had pictured her.

When they entered the Morton house again, and he took a good hard look at her in the light, her face was not quite the keen fresh face which he remembered. Beautiful, yes; and yet there was a certain coarseness about it. Surely it hadn't been like that?

WHILE the two were out, walking in the moonlight, Blackstone Kent had put in a long distance call for Boston, and had informed the surprised district attorney that his missing assistant had been located, and to send operatives at once.

After Helyn had gone to bed, the three men discussed the latest developments. Kent told what he had done.

"Then I must notify the *Post*," exclaimed Larry, jumping up and making for the phone. "If my own paper gets scooped on some news that I myself dug up, why—"

"I'm sorry," said the lawyer. "but it is out of the question. I made the district attorney—he's a very good friend of mine—agree to give out no statement for the present. When he finally does so, he will give it out exclusively through you."

"You're a brick!" said Larry, sitting down again.

"Besides," added Kent, "the telephone is out of order again, and it's I who did the disconnecting this time."

"When will the men from the Department be here?" asked Blakeslee.

"They are taking the night sleeper," replied the lawyer. "They should reach Bretton Woods early to-morrow and join us in a raid on the Jones Lumber Camp."

"But what can three detectives do against that outfit?" objected Larry.

"It will not be merely three detectives," Kent smiled, "but the government of the United States. I hardly believe that the Jones Lumber Camp will care to defy openly one hundred and twenty million people."

CHAPTER XIII

WILD-GOOSE CHASE

JUST BEFORE NOON the next day three burly detectives arrived in Kent's car, which he had sent up to Bretton Woods to meet them. But they soon explained that they would have to wait until morning for the search-warrant.

Blackstone Kent introduced them to Jack Blakeslee and Larrabee. Helyn was not in evidence. Then the six men held a conference in the garden, out in the open, where they could be sure of not being overheard.

Kent and his two allies rapidly narrated to the three visitors all the events that had occurred. To say that the detectives were surprised would he too mild; they were flabbergasted! Only their respect for Blackstone Kent, and their realization of his standing with their boss, the United States District Attorney, prevented them from openly flouting his opinions and his incredible statements of fact. As it was, they exchanged frequent significant glances.

Helyn returned from a walk by herself in the woods, the three strangers were introduced as clients of her father's, and they all went in to lunch.

After lunch Kent took Blakeslee and the three government operatives on a sight-seeing tour, and Larry played around with Helyn. Late in the afternoon the sightseers returned.

Dinner was uneventful. But after dinner an unexpected caller arrived; none other than Aaron Cohen. When the visitor was introduced as "Mr. Washington Jones of the Jones Lumber

Camp," Larry and Jack had great difficulty in concealing their antagonism, and the three detectives were surprised. But "Mr. Jones" did not seem to notice anything amiss.

The handsome young caller appeared to make an immediate impression on Helyn, and did his best to ingratiate himself with her father.

He said that he had called because of the kind invitation of Mr. Kent several evenings ago. Very tactfully he omitted to make any allusion either to the letter or to the disappearance of Miss Kent.

It also appeared that a further object of his call this evening was to make the acquaintance of the two young aviators, who, he understood, had had an accident in the woods just outside the fence of his camp.

He emphasized the word "outside," with a fleeting smile and eye-flash at the angry pair, and continued, "I regret that you did not call at my camp for assistance. We should have given you a hearty welcome. As it is, I took the liberty of having some of my men dismantle your plane and haul it into camp, and shall be delighted to ship it out for you on lumber-trucks, if you will but say the word as to where you wish it delivered."

Jack Blakeslee confusedly mumbled something about the Mt. Washington airport at Bretton Woods.

"It shall be done," said Mr. "Jones" suavely.

The three operatives from the Department of Justice winked covertly at each other.

Once during the evening Helyn made a slip, when she addressed the caller as "Aaron." Kent, Blakeslee, and Larrabee all noticed it, but gave no outward sign that they had done so. Aaron Cohen himself hurriedly made some remark, to cover up the slip.

Finally "Mr. Jones" arose to leave. As he shook hands all round he asked, "By the way, wouldn't you folks like to visit my camp to-morrow morning? I have many modern improvements there, which I am sure will prove both interesting and instructive."

Jack and Larry gasped. The three operatives grinned broadly. To them this was the culmination of an evening of complete disproof of the cock-and-bull story which had brought them up into the New Hampshire woods on a wild-goose chase.

Blackstone Kent alone gave no sign that he felt the offer to be at all unusual. He gravely thanked "Mr. Jones" for his kindness, and assured him that they would all be over in the morning.

With an expression of ill-concealed triumph in his eye, Aaron Cohen, alias Washington Jones, made his departure.

AS SOON as Helyn had gone to bed the three detectives expressed their opinion of the situation in no uncertain terms. Unfortunately they had not noticed when Helyn had referred to "Mr. Jones" as "Aaron," and so they refused to admit that the evening had developed a single hit of evidence tending otherwise than to exonerate the Lumber Camp from any connection whatsoever with the disappearance of Eliot Endicott or to cast suspicion upon it.

Kent, Blakeslee and Larrabee, however, in spite of the incredulity of the Federal operatives, felt that the evening had been a net gain for them, for they now knew definitely who "Aaron" was; and accordingly they were now sure that Helyn had spent at the Jones Lumber Camp the four days of her absence, and had not suffered the lapse of memory which she pretended.

Early the next morning the six men and the girl arrived at the main gate of the Jones Lumber Camp in Kent's car. "Mr. Jones" met them, greeted them effusively, and led them inside. Kent's chauffeur remained outside, with the car pointed away from the camp, and the Department of Justice had been notified to send up a fourth operative, who was to call for immediate help if the seven did not emerge by mid-afternoon.

But all these precautions proved to be unnecessary. Their host showed them through every room of every building of the camp, and there was not a single thing anywhere to indicate

Helyn struck at him with one little fist.

that this was anything other than what it purported to be, namely a very modern and up-to-date lumbering establishment.

There were model barracks for the men, a motion picture theater, a fully equipped hospital, a mess-hall, an administration building, a power house, and extensive laboratories. The laboratories were explained as being a personal hobby of the rich proprietor of the camp, who combined business with pleasure, by employing an unnecessarily large corps of research physicians to care for the health of his employees, and incidentally carry on their experiments in his laboratories.

Nowhere was there any evidence of the dragon, the huge antman, or the animated golden statue, which the two young flyers had claimed to have seen, nor of the missing Eliot Endicott. There was no searchlight on the tower, nor anywhere else. There were no machine guns. There was no matter-transmitting apparatus. The power house was not wired to the Cyclone fence. No guards patrolled the fence.

The uniform look of animal stupidity on the faces of all the employees was very noticeable, but did not give the visitors any clue.

Kent, Blakeslee and Larrabee were chagrined. The three detectives were almost openly derisive over the triumph of "common sense." Helyn seemed mildly amused at something. "Mr. Jones" was the soul of courtesy.

After the tour of inspection, they all ate with the lumberjacks in the mess-hall. The food was plain but excellent. After luncheon a short picture-show was given for their benefit.

Then they thanked their host for his courtesy, and drove away. Helyn, Larry and Jack were dropped off at Morton's. Then the rest of the party drove to Bretton Woods, where the three detectives were to take the night sleeper back to Boston. On the way, they picked up the fourth Federal man at Bartlett.

There was nothing to be said. Aaron Cohen had won. The operatives asserted that they would feel bound to report to the district attorney that Blackstone Kent had been victimized by a couple of irresponsible and sensation-mongering youths.

Kent gave the operatives an early supper at one of the hotels, then sheepishly bade them good-by.

On the return from Bretton Woods, he took the wheel himself, and drove in gloomy silence with the chauffeur sitting beside him.

As the sun set, and the evening twilight deepened, Kent summed up all the facts with the mind of a trained lawyer. After all, what evidence was there, of which he himself could be sure? Not one single bit, except an envelope which he had seen the first time he had been in Larrabee's room at the Bartlett hotel, and a dead pigeon with a hole in the back of its head, which he had seen when they had gone back for the envelope. All the rest was mere hearsay, inadmissible, based upon the mere say-so of a couple of young harebrains, and most of it upon the mere say-so of Lawrence Larrabee, a newspaper reporter who admitted he was prone to follow wild hunches. Blackstone Kent himself began to share the doubts of the men from the Department of Justice.

Of course, there was the peculiar condition of his daughter Helyn. That was undeniable. But even that was no proof of anything, for it might perfectly well be due to amnesia.

"**HIGGINS**," Kent abruptly asked his chauffeur, "how much do you know about this matter?"

The chauffeur awoke with a start.

"What matter, sir?"

"The Jones Lumber Camp mystery."

"Only that four big bloodhounds did actually chase those two fellows, sir."

"Plaguey little!" grumbled his employer.

But lawyers are essentially partisan. Blackstone Kent was still for his own side of the case. So he cogitated some more in silence.

It occurred to him that the matter-transmitting apparatus, if such a thing really existed, might have been quite hard-put to remove all suspicious signs from the Jones camp during the brief period between the time this "Aaron" person learned of the arrival of the three detectives, and their tour of inspection of the camp. By Jove, there was another bit of corroborative evidence, which he had forgotten, namely that he himself had heard Helyn call the man "Aaron." That checked up with the telephone conversation which young Blakeslee claimed to have over heard. At this recollection, he quite brightened up.

Then he continued his line of thought. Some things probably had been actually shipped out of the camp in some normal manner. Certainly the matter-transmitting apparatus must have been so shipped out, for it couldn't transmit itself by wireless!

So when he reached Bartlett, he hunted up the railroad freight-agent, and learned from him the interesting and encouraging news that this very morning the lumber camp trucks had brought down several loads of large and heavy packing-boxes, consigned to Washington Jones, Boston, Mass. Will call."

Upon receiving this information, Kent rushed to a telephone, called the residence of the United States Attorney at Boston, and secured the promise of that official that he would have the shipment investigated immediately upon its arrival.

Very much pleased with himself, Blackstone Kent drove on toward Morton's. But, as he no longer needed a vent for the pent-up irritation which he no longer felt, he yielded the wheel to his chauffeur.

It was now quite dark. On rounding a turn in the road, the headlights suddenly disclosed a huge bloodhound, standing motionless before them, its eyes tightly closed, momentarily blinded by the sudden glare.

Instinctively the chauffeur applied the brakes and tried to steer around the creature, but Blackstone Kent, with a sudden inspiration, kicked the man's foot off the pedal, seized the wheel, and bore down upon the luckless beast.

A moment later the car lay on its side in the ditch, and the two men were crawling out, shaken but unhurt. The dog was writhing and twitching in the center of the road.

"Are you crazy?" exclaimed Higgins angrily.

"Not one bit of it!" his employer exulted. "Quick, catch that dog!"

For the stricken creature was frantically trying to drag its poor crushed body off into the bushes.

Together the two men caught it quite easily. It snapped viciously at them, but was too far gone to be very dangerous. Its struggles became weaker and weaker.

Eagerly Kent examined the back of its head, with a flash light. Yes, there was a scar, just as Larrabee had described it on the pigeon!

The dying dog looked up at them with a piteous expression, almost human. Then it stood up feebly, and tottered around on the dusty road, making most peculiar motions with one of its front feet, finally to fall to the ground again, give one shudder, and then lie still.

KENT and his chauffeur carried the dead form into the glare of the headlights of the wrecked car. And there the lawyer whipped out his knife, and carved hurriedly into the back of the creature's skull. He was on what lawyers call a "fishing expedition"—following on mere hunch a line of evidence with no very definite idea as to where it would lead.

It led to a small squirming white grub, which Kent wrapped carefully in a handkerchief, and placed in his pocket. Then they carried the body back and laid it where it had been hit by the car. To conceal the fact of the post-mortem which he had performed, Kent bashed in the creature's skull with a stone.

As he swept his flash light around about his handiwork, his eyes lit upon the peculiar marks the dog's paw had made in the dust of the road.

"What do you make of those, Higgins?" he asked.

"I don't know, sir," was the reply. "They do look like shorthand, don't they?"

"They do to me," asserted Kent. "Let's copy them."

So, handing the light to his man, the lawyer took out his notebook and duplicated the marks as well as he could. Then he rubbed out the originals with his foot.

Blackstone Kent's confidence in the justice of his side of the case of *Larrabee et al.* vs. *Jones* was now fully restored.

By the time that the two men, on foot, reached Morton's, every one else was in bed.

The next morning, Kent phoned to the Bartlett garage to come and get the wrecked car. The body of the dead bloodhound had disappeared during the night, Kent ascertained by later inquiring of the garage man.

At the first opportunity, the lawyer took his daughter aside, and suddenly flashed at her the writing in his notebook.

"Where did you get that?" she exclaimed, caught off her guard.

"I rather thought you would be interested," he replied. "Do you know what it means?"

"Why—no," she said in a puzzled tone, as though trying to decipher it; then suddenly, her face flushing. "Of course not. Why should I? You know I don't understand shorthand."

Her father snapped the book shut, and returned it to his pocket, well satisfied that the girl had recognized the writing as a code with which she ought to be familiar, but which she had not yet had enough experience to be able to read.

As soon as he could get the two boys out of earshot of Helyn, he recounted to them his latest bits of evidence, and showed them the moth-grub, by now unfortunately deceased.

He also showed it to Helyn, and elicited a momentary embarrassed flash of recognition.

But there is seldom any progress without some set-back. The district attorney phoned him from Boston to say that, after hearing the full report of the three operatives, he must emphatically decline to follow any more of Kent's harebrained hunches. Accordingly the shipment of freight would remain unmolested.

Blackstone Kent retorted that he still believed in the facts which he had reported, which statement immediately brought down upon his head considerable scornful abuse.

Kent grimly reported the phone conversation to his two guests.

Larry's comment was, "I don't see why the district attorney should be angry at you, Mr. Kent. You're entitled to your opinion."

"No, I'm not," snapped Kent. "No one is. My boy, one of the fundamental principles of life, which I have learned from my long experience with the world, is that no one is entitled to his opinion—that is to say, not in the eyes of any one else."

At any rate, they knew they could expect no further assistance from the skeptical Department of Justice. Then Larry resource-fully called the *Post*, and got them to set a reporter to trace what was done with the freight on its arrival. But "Jones" and his agents were too clever. The reporter could find no trace of the packages, which must have been spirited away successfully.

CHAPTER XIV

THE ENEMY STRIKES!

THEN ENSUED SEVERAL days of marking time, during which "Washington Jones"—Cohen—called frequently upon Helyn Kent, and the girl flirted outrageously both with him and Lawrence Larrabee. Larry and Jack Blakeslee were still guests of the Kents.

But Blackstone Kent himself was not wasting all this time. He was studying his daughter as he had never before studied even his most important witnesses.

Finally he confided in Larry.

"Larrabee," Kent said gloomily, "I cannot believe that this girl is my daughter. She looks like Helyn exactly, or I would think she was a double, an actress planted upon me as a spy. She doesn't act like Helyn. Her mind does not react in the way Helyn's used to. And yet she remembers every incident of Helyn's past life. I can't understand it. My poor little girl!"

"I agree with you, Mr. Kent," the reporter admitted thoughtfully. "This Helyn seems to me to be quite a different person from the girl whom I admired on the train."

"The only physical change is that she wears her hair differently," Kent pointed out. "Have you noticed that barrette at the back? But of course you wouldn't. Anyway, she never wore a barrette before the day she disappeared." He paused; then a sudden light gleamed in his eyes, and he continued, "See here, Larry. Act awkward and knock it off some time, and then look sharply underneath."

Larry was frankly puzzled.

"I don't understand what you mean, but I'll do it."

Kent gave a wry smile of inward amusement mingled with pain, but refused to explain any further.

The opportunity came that very evening. Larry and Helyn were seated together on the sofa. She rose for some purpose; and, as he rose with her out of politeness, he suddenly pretended to stumble. Clutching for something by which to steady himself, he reached out one hand gropingly, and swept the ornament from her hair.

Then he gasped with horror.

Helyn wheeled, and struck at him with one little fist, her face white with rage. Then snatching up the barrette, and bursting into tears, she fled from the room. Nor did she put in an appearance again all that evening.

LARRY at once sought out Blackstone Kent.

As Larry approached, with a look of mingled triumph and horror on his face, the older man halted him with upraised hand.

"Don't tell me what you discovered," said he sadly. "Let *me* tell *you*. My daughter has a scar on the back of her head, like the pigeon, and the cat, and the dog. She's my own daughter—under a ghastly spell—and no impersonator."

"But what's to be done about it?" asked Larry.

"My natural inclination," replied Blackstone Kent, "would be to send at once for either an expert surgeon, or a noted psychiatrist, or both. I almost feel she'd be better dead than a slave of these creatures."

"Well, why not?"

"Simply because Helvn, being under the spell of those diabolical criminals, headed by Washington Jones, or Aaron Jones, or whatever his name is, would certainly refuse to submit to either a physical or a mental examination."

"Couldn't she be taken by surprise and by force?"

"Not a chance," replied Kent glumly. "The moment we sent for the doctors, the enemy would learn of it, and would warn Helyn."

"May I then suggest a plan?" asked Larry. "Sir Francis Moxon is staying at Bretton Woods."

"And who is he?"

"London's most brilliant brain surgeon. Furthermore, and fortunately for our plans, he is unknown here. He has registered simply as Francis Moxon, and no one is paying him the least attention, which is just what he wants, for he's here on a vacation."

"Then how do *you* know who he is?"

"Once, when I was just a cub reporter," replied Larrabee, "I covered some sort of a meeting at the Harvard Medical School, and met him there. The other day, while Jack and I were waiting for the weather to clear, so that we could borrow Carson's plane, I ran across Sir Francis. He recognized me, but begged me not to tell who he was, as he's over here in America for a complete rest. We had quite a chat, and I know that he would drop his incognito in an instant, for such an interesting case as this terrible affair promises to afford."

"I'll run up to Bretton Woods tomorrow," exclaimed Blackstone Kent, "for a day of golf, and bring Sir Francis back with me to dinner."

"Are you going to tell him all about what we know, and what we suspect?" asked Larrabee.

"Yes. Why not?"

"But will he believe such a preposterous tale?"

"I think so," asserted Kent thoughtfully. "You must remember that he is a scientist, not a detective. Scientists are apt to be open-minded."

"Better invite that Aaron Washington Jones person to dinner, too," advised Larry.

"You aren't serious, are you?" demanded the lawyer.

"Yes, I am," the reporter asserted. "Invite him, and hope he doesn't accept. Then we'll know where he is."

"A good idea!" exclaimed Kent. "I'll do it."

BY THE next morning Helyn had recovered her poise. She accepted at its face value her father's suggestion that Mr. Jones be invited to dinner. So she attempted to get in touch with him, only to find that he was to be out of town for several days. Her father departed, ostensibly for his golf, leaving instructions not to wait dinner if he didn't show up in time.

Jack and Larry kept their eyes on Helyn all day. So far as they could see, she communicated with neither man nor beast.

Her father returned just in time for dinner, bringing with him an unexpected guest, whose name Helyn didn't quite catch, but whom her father introduced as a man with whom he had been paired at golf. Helyn was used to her father's golf friendships, which had been many and brief.

The guest was pleasant enough, but somewhat stupid. He talked very little to any one except Mr. Kent, and that little consisted in a comparison of trick holes at various courses throughout the United States. Apparently the gentleman, whoever he was, had golfed extensively.

Kent addressed him as "Frank," and he called his host "Blackie." The two younger men and Helyn paid him very little attention, devoting their conversation to each other.

After dinner, coffee was served in the living room.

The servant had scarcely withdrawn, when Helyn took a sip from her cup, let it crash to the floor, and keeled over unconscious.

Instantly their guest shed his sleepy manner. Forgotten was his assumed interest in golf. He became professional and alert. He and Blackstone carried the unconscious girl upstairs. They carried her to her father's room so that there would be no undue activity in her room, for the servants to notice. In her own room, they put on the lights, drew the shades, and closed the door. By prearrangement, Jack and Larry remained in the living room.

There was not a possibility of any one, except the four of them, knowing of Helen's having been drugged, for the curtains in the living room had all been down, and the servants had all been in their own part of the house.

When the maid came to get the cups and saucers, the two young men were to mention casually that Helyn had spilled some coffee on her dress and had gone to her room, and that Mr. Kent had taken his new friend upstairs, to show him some golf clothes.

The two tried to read magazines. The maid came for the dishes. Their program of explanations went through as planned. They gave it added plausibility by ringing for the maid to wipe up the mess, and by telling her that Mr. Kent had said for them to do so, just as he departed to show "this Frank person" his new knickers.

Then ensued the weary suspense of waiting. It seemed hours; but really it probably was not over thirty minutes.

At last Blackstone Kent and Sir Francis returned, both looking very solemn.

"She has come out of the anæsthetic and is asleep," reported the surgeon.

Her father held up, for their inspection, a small white grub, wriggling between his thumb and forefinger. Then, with an exclamation of disgust, he threw it on the hearth and stamped it it.

Sir Francis reached out to stop him, but was too late.

"Lost to science!" said he resignedly.

"There'll be plenty more of these for science, before I get through," announced Blackstone Kent grimly.

HELYN slept in her own room that night. Her father sat up all night in his room, and made frequent trips in to see if she was all right. The girl slept late in the morning, but that was nothing unusual. The golf-guest stayed on, but that, too, was not out of the ordinary.

It was a distraught father and an anxious surgeon who awaited Helyn's awakening. Would she be cured? Would she be sane? If the two men had known more about the system of Whoomang new-souls, they would have been even more worried. In fact, they might never have dared to operate.

The younger men went for a long brisk walk. Anything to get away from the maddening suspense. While they were gone, Helyn awoke.

Sir Francis let Kent go in to her alone.

For a few minutes she lay quietly with her eyes open, a puzzled look on her face. She did not notice her father. Then she felt of her bandages, and murmured something which sounded like, "Once before." And then she saw her father, and smiled.

Quickly he came to her bed and knelt beside it. With a glad little cry she flung her arms around his shoulders and wept, while he patted her and said, "My little girl! My little girl!"

After a while she stopped her sobbing and lay back on the pillows again.

"Oh, father," said she faintly, "I'm so ashamed. Can you ever forgive me? Pretty soon I'll tell you everything, but I'm too tired now."

"My poor darling," he replied brokenly, "there's nothing to forgive."

It was a trite and banal sentiment, but it came from the heart.

All day long she refused to let her father leave her side. Sir Francis Moxon slipped in from his room, from time to time, when there was none to see. No one else was admitted. The statement was given out to the household that she had bumped her head quite badly during the night.

The next day it was stated that she had caught a bad cold. The old doctor from the village came and actually treated her for a cold, the necessary symptoms being supplied by rouging the edges of her nose and by using a hot mouthwash shortly before her temperature was taken. By this time her only bandage was a small one at the back of her head, which was not visible when she lay on her pillow.

Sir Francis Moxon returned to Bretton Woods, subject to call.

Helyn's convalescence took longer than had been required after her original operation among the Whoomangs. As she convalesced, she gradually told her father all that she knew about Boomalayla, Doggo, Quivven, and Aaron Cohen. She told of their dream of empire, and the fiendish system moth-grub souls, and the huge organization which they were building up, with thousands of "robot" reserves—corpses in water-glass storage. She told them that they had made a Whoomang out of Eliot Endicott. Kent and Blakeslee and Larrabee were horrified.

"We must get you out of here at once," her father repeatedly insisted.

But each time she would reply, "Where is your old spirit, dad? We must fight this menace together, you and I."

At first she had suggested warning the world, but Blackstone Kent had learned his lesson from his sad experience with the incredulity of the three operatives from the Department of Justice. He knew that any attempt to warn the world would result merely in a questioning of his sanity, perhaps even in his being locked up.

No, the three of them, he and Jack and Larry, must match their wits against this organization with its superhuman science.

To which Helve added, "Not the three of you, father; but the four of us.

Finally he yielded to her insistence.

Sometimes she would startle him by momentarily resuming her old Whoomang expression.

"Don't look at me like that, Helyn!" he would exclaim. "You frighten me."

But she would reply, "I must practice it, father."

Lawrence Larrabee was overjoyed to find his "girl of the

train" recreated, and spent many hours at her bedside; and Jack Blakeslee, too, was most attentive.

It was Larry, however, who proved to be the devoted suitor. With true Irish impetuosity he made love to Helyn, and conducted such a whirlwind campaign as to result, within very few days, in their engagement. But, on account of tactical considerations, the happy news was announced only to Blackstone Kent and Jack Blakeslee.

AARON COHEN returned from his trip, and called, and was admitted to see her. It was a trying ordeal for the girl, but she weathered it.

When he had gone, she reported, "Aaron doesn't suspect a thing, and I have learned a lot. He has just been on a tour of inspection of all the headquarters of the Whoomang organization. Everything is in fine shape. They will be ready to strike in about two months, although the exact date has not yet been set. When that day comes, they plan to overthrow the government of America. Aaron wants me to keep you out of the way, and I promised to do it."

"All right," replied her father, "let's move. The Mortons are due back here anyway, in about a week. And certainly the activities of this particular lumber camp have been abandoned. Where is the chief headquarters of the triumvirate now?"

"Aaron wouldn't tell me," answered the girl. "Not that he mistrusts me, for he thinks I am one of them; but he fears your detective ability, father."

So the Kents left Morton's and returned to their Cambridge apartment. Jack Blakeslee resumed his interrupted airplane tour. Lawrence Larrabee reported back to the Boston *Post,* and was promptly fired—by request, but nobody except the editor and himself knew that. He secured a small job on an inconspicuous Florida newspaper, and dropped out of the picture.

As Cohen's organization had no operations in Florida as yet, Larry ceased to worry them. Helyn received occasional brief letters—quite guardedly written—from the young reporter,

which she promptly forwarded to Aaron Cohen. Also she reported to Cohen that her father had given up the case in disgust,
disbelieving the fantastic stories of the reporter and his friend
Blakeslee.

Cohen's agents reported much the same thing of Kent's
activities.

And then Blackstone Kent was called to London, to help
organize a British subsidiary for one of his American corpora-
tion clients.

Aaron Cohen and his criminals had free rein once more.

Yet still Aaron refused to give any information to Helyn.
Some sixth sense must have warned him. As long as Blackstone
Kent was on earth, the shrewd conspirators feared and mis-
trusted him. So he planted one of his best spies on Kent's ship.

But this last worry was shortly thereafter removed. The spy
radioed in code that he had pushed Kent overboard the first
day out, and this was confirmed by news items to the effect that
Blackstone Kent, New England's leading criminal lawyer, was
missing from his stateroom and had presumably fallen into the
sea; that he had complained to the ship's doctor of feeling dizzy,
and so probably had had a fainting spell when near the rail.

Helyn was prostrated, but being the true child of her father
that she was, determined to carry on, and at once communicated with Cohen, saying, "Now I can come to you, and stay
with you without fear."

Her message crossed one from Aaron, directing her to report
at a certain Boston address, so as to be transmitted by radio to
the new headquarters of the organization. But she delayed
several days, ostensibly to close up the apartment and put the
furniture in storage, but actually to give herself time to recover
sufficiently from her grief so as to be able to face the man whom
she believed responsible for her father's death. For the stricken
girl's heart was heavy with grief.

Meanwhile Lawrence Larrabee, down in Florida, read the
news of Kent's death with horror. His first impulse was to rush

to his fiancée, to comfort her. But then, he reflected, this would undo all the good that he had hoped to accomplish by his enforced retirement, namely, lulling of the enemy into a false sense of security so far as he was concerned.

Now that Kent was dead, it was up to Larry to carry on. The very feeling of safety which the news would give to Aaron Cohen and his organization would make them all the less likely to put a watch on one little discredited newspaper reporter. So he merely sent Helyn a heartfelt note of sincere condolence.

Jack Blakeslee, at one of the Southern flying fields, also read the sad news. Like his friend Larry, he had been idly marking time, waiting for instructions from Blackstone Kent, instructions which now would never come. So he turned his plane toward Florida, to hunt up the reporter. The two of them must take up the fight, at the point to which their recently stricken leader had carried it.

The very day that Jack reached the little town where Larry was working, the latter received a note, which had been mailed by Blackstone Kent just before he sailed. It came now, like a voice from the dead, and would have served to determine their course if they had needed any final stimulus. It was short, concise and very much to the point, it read:

If anything should happen to me, you two must carry on!

CHAPTER XV

LIFE AMONG THE ROBOTS

ABOUT A MONTH later two ragged young men, with pinched, unshaven laces, sat in a cheap restaurant in Birmingham, eating a meager meal and eagerly scanning the want-ads in the *Age Herald*. All day long they had tramped the streets, looking for work. From office to office they had gone, without landing a job, and now they were about to return for another night in the ten-cent flophouse where they were staying.

The strange thing about it all was that they had actually received offers of employment at several places which they had visited that day, offers which it would seem they ought to have accepted in view of their present almost penniless condition. But the work had apparently not been to their liking, for they had turned it down. They were still without a job.

"Do you suppose," asked one, "that some one of these places which we have passed up is actually Theirs?"

"Do you suppose," countered the other, "that They haven't any office in this city?"

"If They haven't," replied the first pseudo-job-hunter, "then all I can say is that Birmingham's boast to being one of the principal cities of America is all hooey. For They are supposed to have an office in every principal city!"

"Well, anyway," said the other, "let's call it a day, and go to a show. We're entitled to some fun out of life, you know."

So together the two ragged youths went to a movie.

After the show, on the way out, one of them suddenly clutched the other's arm.

"Look!" he gasped.

Going past the door of the theater was a young man of about their own age, but as prosperous as they were poverty-stricken, a young man with an unforgettable, ambitious expression. Furtively the two youths followed him until he entered one of the leading hotels.

After a reasonable wait, one of them remained on guard outside, while the other boldly entered and studied the register. Before the clerk noticed him and got the bell-captain to eject him, he had run through the register for quite a way back. But he had not found any familiar name.

Outside again, he reported to his comrade. The two of them then hung around within sight of the doors until well after midnight, but the man whom they had followed did not come out again.

Early the next morning they were again at their post. Around eight thirty, their quarry emerged, and they followed him. He went straight to a near-by office building, took the elevator, and entered a door marked, "Southern Land Company, Ltd."

So the two hastened down to the ground-floor again, and bought a morning paper. Sure enough, the Southern Land Company, Ltd., was advertising for common laborers.

"That's the place!" exclaimed one of them. "Let's go!"

But the other wasn't so sure. So they hung around the building for a couple of hours. Then, as the man failed to come out again, they bought an additional paper, and went up one by one to apply for work, each carrying a copy of the want ad.

A dull-faced old man questioned them, asking particularly about their relatives. When they both disclaimed having any, they were promptly hired. Once, during the interview, they caught sight of the man whom they had followed.

When all the preliminaries had been completed, they were

taken by trolley, with about twenty other new employees, to a house in the suburbs.

IT WAS an ordinary enough house in appearance, except that in the yard stood two tall towers of steel lattice-work, supporting an aërial. One of the newly employed men nudged the other, and they both glanced upward and smiled. This, then, was their journey's end!

It proved, rather, to be their journey's beginning. One by one the new employees were led into a room full of electrical apparatus, and were ordered to sit down on the floor in a small curtained inclosure. Those who objected, were forced to do it at the point of a pistol. There was a strong smell of ozone in the air. From time to time a man in a smock, standing at a switch-panel, closed certain switches. None of the employees who had entered the curtained cubicle ever came out again.

But none of them realized that they never came out again. It seemed to each of them that he came out again quite quickly, but that while he had been inside the cubicle, it had been moved to somewhere else. And when they were led from the house again, it turned out to be a strange house, located in the midst of some woods. The hour seemed a bit earlier in the day than it had been in Birmingham, and the weather was decidedly cooler.

From the building, the men were led to a dental establishment, where their teeth were promptly filled under an instantaneous anæsthetic with no aftermath of nausea. Then they were assigned cots in a bunk house, and were issued uniform shirts and overalls.

Most of them were so dazed by the whole performance that they submitted meekly.

The first thing that the two young men did, upon reaching the privacy of the bunk house, was to examine the backs of each other's heads. Apparently satisfied with what they found, or rather didn't find there, they fished in their pockets for something. Then their faces fell in ludicrous dismay.

"My razor is gone!" exclaimed Larry. "Yet I'm sure it was there just before we got into the matter-transmitting apparatus, for I felt of it on purpose to make certain that everything was O.K."

"Mine's gone, too!" cried Jack. "Why, that queers the whole game!"

Helyn had omitted to tell them that the matter-transmitting apparatus always left metallic objects behind.

Jack and Larry looked at each other in despair. All their best-laid plans had come to naught. Each had had a scar made on the back of his head, before they had started to look for work. Their plan had been to shave the hair away from the scar, upon arrival at wherever they were shipped to, and then try and palm themselves off as newly-made Whoomangs. Without razors, this was impossible. What could they do now, to avert the danger of being operated on and actually becoming helpless, will-less Whoomangs?

It would do no good to try and borrow a razor from any of their shack-mates, for these were all newcomers like themselves, and hence like themselves would undoubtedly have lost their own razors in the same inexplicable manner. They were indeed in desperate straits!

Their only hope, and that was a slim one, lay in borrowing a razor from one of the guards. Such an attempt might secure them a razor, but it would also serve to call them to the guard's attention, and impress upon him their appearance, so that he would be likely to miss them when they skipped out. Nevertheless, the chance must be taken, for it was their only hope.

The guard was a gray-haired man, who looked as though he had once been a gentleman, but had been beaten down by hard luck and perhaps dissipation. He was tall, but walked with a stoop. There was a certain masked keenness in his dull animal-like eyes.

JACK approached him diffidently, and said, "Say, buddy, they fixed our teeth. Can't we get a shave, too, somewhere around here?"

The guard looked sharply at Jack, seemed to be reading the erstwhile aviator's mind, and yet continued to keep his face absolutely expressionless.

"No," he growled, "you can't."

The guard's voice sounded strangely familiar. Jack returned the man's stare. Where had he seen that face before? His fear of recognition grew, but he persisted.

"Could yer loan us yours, buddy?" he asked. "I want to look nice, so's I'll be sure and hold my job."

"You'll hold your job, all right," replied the guard grimly. "No, I won't lend you my razor. You might hurt somebody with it."

Then bending suddenly close to Blakeslee, he whispered, "I have a better plan. Wait until after supper. Your physical examination isn't scheduled until to-morrow, so you have plenty or time."

And, with this cryptic remark, he strode away. What could he possibly mean? Bewildered, Jack returned to his bunk, to report to Larrabee.

All the rest of the day, the new employees sat around in the bunk house. They were not permitted to leave the building. A curious menace pervaded the atmosphere, but no one except Larry and Jack appeared to notice it.

They were not even permitted to leave for meals. Instead, tin plates and cups were distributed to them, and some dull-faced workmen brought pots of steaming coffee and kettles of slum.

The gray-haired guard passed by the bunks of the two new-comers several times during the day, but appeared to be studying Larry intently, rather than Jack. This was strange, as it was Jack who had asked him for the razor! To Larry, as well as Jack, there was something vaguely familiar about the guard.

Finally the guard came and sat on Larry's bed. The reporter had great difficulty in concealing his concern.

While he was concentrating on an effort to appear calm, the

guard suddenly leaned forward and whispered in his ear, "Have you a scar on the back of your head?"

"Yes," replied Larry, taken completely by surprise.

Then he bit his lip, but it was too late.

"And has Jack?" continued the guard.

"Say, who the devil are *you?*" he blurted out.

"Sh!" admonished the guard. "You'll have to do better than this. Apparently my disguise is perfect. Yours is pretty good, and I might not have recognized either of you, if Jack hadn't asked for a loan of my razor."

"But who are you?" persisted Larrabee.

The guard smiled.

"Oh," said he. "I'm Blackstone Kent."

He beckoned Jack Blakeslee over to the cot, and repeated the statement, then cautioned them to silence. Both were completely stunned by the news.

"Everything's all right," he asserted. "Wait for me here this evening," and he arose and left.

The two plotters were flabbergasted. So Kent had been kidnaped, instead of thrown overboard! Kent was now a Whoomang, and they were in his power. What hope now to save America from the enemy?

Jack Blakeslee and Lawrence Larrabee passed the rest of the afternoon in deep gloom.

AFTER supper, after it was dark, Kent came. Another Whoomang was now on guard. Kent told the boys to gather up their belongings, and cautioned them to be very discreet and to look their dumbest, for their lives and even the whole future of the race might depend upon what happened during the next few minutes.

Their fears were well-founded, for the guard stopped them.

"Where are you taking those two new men?" he asked truculently.

"These aren't *new* men," Kent explained. "They belong to the organization. They were shipped here from another camp, and got sent down to this barracks by mistake. I just received orders to move them over to the guard barracks."

Would the Whoomang believe this? Apparently not, for he growled, "Prove it!"

Kent sighed, as though exasperated; then said resignedly, "Show him your heads, bohunks. I assume you have new-souls like the rest of us."

It was surprisingly simple. They did have the external evidence of souls, namely scars at the base of the skull. The guard let them through.

Kent took them promptly to a dark portion of the camp, and there in whispers told them what had happened.

He had gone off the ship before it sailed. But first he had left a note for the steward to call him at a certain hour the next morning. Then he had sent himself a radiogram of *bon voyage*, from the shore. The unslept-in condition of his berth, and the failure of the steward to find him anywhere on board to deliver the radiogram, had undoubtedly resulted in the impression that he had been drowned.

"But how about the ship's surgeon saying that you complained to him of dizziness?" objected Larrabee.

"So I did," replied Kent, "but he evidently forgot that it happened before sailing. So here I am, and Aaron Cohen never suspects. Why, I have even learned that a spy whom he planted on the ship sent a message that he had pushed me overboard. Faking the story, so as to get a little undeserved praise, I guess. Anyway it helped a lot."

Then the lawyer's face sobered, and he continued, "Poor little Helyn. I suppose my death broke her all up. But I didn't dare let even her know."

"I suppose it did hit her pretty hard," said Larry. "But neither of us has seen her, since your death. We didn't dare take a chance either. You told us to carry on, and so here we are."

"But how did you escape having a moth-grub planted in your brain?" asked Jack. "That is, if you really did escape."

"The same plan that you had in mind," replied Kent. "Ever since we all separated, I have been trying to locate one of their offices. It was my discovery of their New York office that determined me on my fake death at sea. Before leaving the boat, I changed into old clothes and shaved off my mustache. From the boat I went directly to a cheap hotel. Then for several days I let my beard grow, and changed gradually to worse and worse clothes, and drifted into more and more disreputable lodgings. Finally I applied to the Whoomangs for work, and was accepted. They shipped me here by radio. By the way, do you know what part of the United States this is?"

"No," they admitted.

"The north woods of Wisconsin," Kent replied.

"But you haven't yet told us how you avoided the operation." Larry persisted.

"I had the scar made, even before going on the boat," said Kent. "Ran across Sir Francis in Boston, played some golf with him at Oakley and got him to do the job. Brought a razor with me, the same as you boys undoubtedly did. But, of course, I lost it *en route*, for that matter-transmitting apparatus can't transmit metals. So here I was, in a perfect pickle, just like you two."

"**WHAT** on earth did you do?" Larry demanded with news-gathering instinct.

"Very simple," Kent replied. "I picked out the most nosey-looking individual among the new employees, and told him enough about the moth-grub new-souls system to get him thoroughly frightened. The result was that, in less than an hour, every one in the bunk house knew of the menace, and was scared to death. That evening men tried to rush the guards. It was quite a riot, with a good many casualties on both sides. I took a revolver off a dead guard, lined up on the side of the authorities, and helped put down the mutiny.

"When it was all over, I marched back to the guard barracks

with the guards. The Whoomangs naturally tried to find out who had started the trouble, but every one pointed to the man whom I had told; and, as he happened to have been killed in the scrimmage, no one suspected me. It was several days before the excitement died down, and by that time I was so familiar a figure in the guard barracks that I was taken for granted. Since then I've been promoted to sergeant, because of being a pretty good shot. By the way, my name is Sergeant Stone. You can remember it by its being the last part of my first name. Your names had better be—well, Larry Lawrence and John Blake wouldn't be bad. An alias wants to be a fairly familiar name to its owner."

Then he led the two men to the guard quarters, where he had bunks, blankets and automatics issued to them.

It was surprising how easy it was for them to drop into the routine of Whoomang life, and to copy the dull looks and robot mannerisms of their associates. Their lack of familiarity with their duties did not give them away, for the duties were simple, and the orders usually explicit.

Kent, Larrabee and Blakeslee—alias Sergeant Stone, and Privates Lawrence and Blake—saw as little of each other as possible, so as to avoid exciting any suspicion; but all kept their eyes and ears open.

Yet they learned practically nothing. The triumvirate were not located at this camp, nor was Aaron Cohen. No one seemed to know or care where these officials were, nor would it do ask. Here they were, hopelessly shunted onto a sidetrack.

Meanwhile a growing conviction spread through the Whoomangs that the day was rapidly approaching when they were to take over the government of the United States. Their dull faces all became lighted with just a touch of excitement and jubilation.

One day Jack Blakeslee disappeared. Just vanished, that was all. His two friends did not dare inquire, for Whoomangs never question their superiors; and thus an inquiry would brand them as not being Whoomangs. Furthermore any undue interest in Jack might betray them as being friends of his.

So they could merely guess and wait for possible catastrophe.

Had he been suspected and discovered? If so, it might be their own turn any moment. And then what fate would lie in store for them? And for Helyn? And for America?

The suspense was made even worse by what Helyn had told them of Swami Singh and his power to tap the human mind; for, if Jack was in his clutches, no amount of self-control could keep him from betraying his fellow-spies.

CHAPTER XVI

THE WAGES OF TREASON

NEW EMPLOYEES KEPT pouring into camp, and all this time the hospital ran night and day, implanting moth-grub souls. The storehouses were piled full with dormant human bodies in water-glass.

Then there came a change. No more men were put in storage. Instead, the work of resuscitating the dormant bodies was begun. All hands were put to work building barracks and re-suscitation-hospitals. Shipments of rifles and ammunition began to arrive, and to fill up the storehouses from which the bodies were being taken.

Kent and Larrabee could envision these same activities taking place at hundreds of such establishments at strategic points throughout the country; but, even so, they could not figure how these untrained hordes could be a match for the Army, Navy and Marines of the United States. Nevertheless the absolute certainty of victory, felt by every Whoomang, could not fail to cast a chill over the two of them. There must be more to the plans of the triumvirate than Kent and Larrabee even suspected.

And meanwhile what had become of their fellow-spy, Jack Blakeslee? And how was Helyn making out? Of course, when they had enlisted, they had cut themselves off from any possible communication with her. She did not even know that her father was alive.

They did not doubt that she was active, and that some day

they would learn of her activities. But when, and where, and how? It was most maddening for the two men who loved her.

At last one day they saw her. Aaron Cohen, Dr. Victor Chapin, and several others, arrived by wireless on a countrywide tour of inspection, and each brought his woman with him. That is to say, Aaron brought Helyn, and the doctor brought his pretty head nurse.

Kent and Larry hung around as much and as often as they could without attracting attention, but found no opportunity to speak to Helyn alone, or even to make their presence known to her. They did, however, get plenty of chances to study her face, and what they saw in it did not reassure them.

It was the dull face of a Whoomang once more. Nor were her actions any more reassuring. Her every gesture, every motion of her beautiful body, was full of moronically sex-conscious appeal to her male companion. She fitted exactly into the same category as that of Dr. Chapin's pet nurse. Her father and her sweetheart were shocked, disgusted and horrified. Had the operation performed by Sir Francis Moxon gone for naught? Had another moth-grub soul been implanted at the base of Helyn's brain?

More days wept by. No news of Jack Blakeslee. No further news of Helyn. Then came Blackstone Kent's opportunity to communicate with the outside world, for he was sent to town on some errand or other of his masters. Fortunately he was given enough foreknowledge of the trip to enable him to write a long letter to the U.S. District Attorney at Boston. And the big shipments of war munitions gave him his excuse to reopen the subject.

So he wrote out a long and complete report, urged the district attorney to send detectives at once, cautioned him not to attempt to reply, and informed him that all future reports would be signed merely "X," so as to avoid detection. Kent figured that the mere fact that his letter would disprove his supposed death at sea, would be sufficient to stir the Department of Justice into renewed activity.

ABOUT a week later, the triumvirate arrived at this Wisconsin camp. There were Boomalayla the dragon, Doggo the antman, and Quivven the golden princess. Also their staff, including Aaron Cohen, Victor Chapin, Rajindra Singh, the *swami*, Chapin's assistant, Dr. Ronk, Dr. Polakowski, and others. Also Goldenflame's prince consort, namely, the renegade assistant district attorney, Eliot Endicott. And, of course, Aaron Cohen's Helyn, and Dr. Chapin's pretty little Whoomang nurse.

Truckloads of electrical apparatus arrived by freight. It was evident that the big drive was about to begin, and that this particular camp was to be the G.H.Q. for the drive. Kent reported all these developments to the Boston District Attorney, signing the letter " X" as prearranged. But it was most tantalizing not to know whether his letters were being acted upon, or even received.

He and Larry decided that one of them, and one only, should make the fateful attempt to speak to Helyn, on the chance that her Whoomang attitude was purely pretended. Larry was chosen for this job, for two reasons: first, because it was more important for the brilliant and influential Kent to survive, if one of them should have to be sacrificed; and secondly, because for Kent to reveal himself to his daughter, who believed him dead, might give her such a shock as to cause her involuntarily to betray herself.

Larry soon found an opportunity. Sent to the administration building to get the outgoing mail, he happened to run across Helyn in the corridor.

"Please, ma'am, just a word with you in private," said he.

She stopped and looked furtively around. This reassured him.

Stepping closer, he whispered, "Show no surprise. I'm Larry."

For an instant a purely human look flashed across her beautiful face; then it resumed its robot-expression.

"Oh, my darling!" she breathed. "Meet me at eight o'clock to-night behind Storehouse No. 9."

Larry reported jubilantly to Kent, but the latter wasn't quite so sure.

"It may be a trap," said he. "Go cautiously. And, even if and when you are satisfied that she is still human, don't tell her about either Jack or me. Poor Jack! I wonder where he is."

That night Larry and Helyn met in the darkness behind Storehouse No. 9. They embraced long and passionately. But neither could see the other's face.

"If this is a trap," murmured Larry, to himself, "it is worth it."

He paused, half expecting to hear the footfalls of approaching guards.

"Do you know," said the girl soberly, "I also feared a trap. Yet I risked it for love of you."

"You're a darling!" breathed her lover.

"But, Larry, dear," she questioned, "if you are a Whoomang, how is it that you are not loyal to the organization, rather than to me? And, if you are not a Whoomang, how is it that you are here unsuspected in their ranks?"

"I am *not* a Whoomang," he replied, "but I have a fake scar, and it has got me by, so far.... Now call out your guards."

"We are putting our heads in the lion's mouth by talking to each other," said she. "But we love each other, and must trust each other, for the sake of each other, and of America."

He kissed her hungrily.

FINALLY she said, "We have no time for love. Our country is at stake. One week from to-day the organization will strike."

"But how can the organization hope to cope with all the military forces of our country?"

"They do not merely hope," said she. "They have supreme confidence. There is not a vessel of the fleet nor a regiment of the Army that has not at least one high officer who has been

Incoherent with fear and jealous rage, she
babbled out her story of treachery.

secretly operated on and made a Whoomang. These robot officers have been sowing the seeds of sedition among their men.
The Whoomangs have Congressmen and Senators of both
political parties. Even the President's Cabinet contains two
Whoomangs. When 'The Day' arrives, the President himself is
to be kidnaped. They will at once proclaim Aaron Cohen as
Emperor of America, and will depend upon these planted men
to drive the Army and Navy to allegiance, or to temporary
ineffectiveness. Besides, our scientists have perfected a death-
ray, with which one man can withstand a whole army. All of
our death-ray machines except one, which is here in this camp,
are now stored in a house in Washington, D.C., ready for use,
when our troops seize the capital."

But what can we do to stop it?" Larry gasped.

"Oh, if father were only still alive!" exclaimed Helyn.

"He—" began Larry, then checked himself. This still might
be a trap. He must be cautious.

But the girl ignored the interruption, and continued, "I have written repeated letters to the authorities reporting everything, and warning them. But I am afraid that it is all too preposterous for them to believe."

A cloaked figure suddenly rounded the corner of the building and almost bumped into the absorbed, whispering pair.

LARRY and Helyn jumped apart with a gasp as the cloaked figure came to an abrupt halt. Without another word the two conspirators fled wildly in different directions into the darkness of the camp. The intruder, whom they saw to be a woman, did not pursue them nor did she call the guards.

Larry reached the guard barracks safely, though out of breath, and drew Kent to one side, telling him what Helyn had said. Blackstone Kent's face fell.

"Now they'll never believe!" he exclaimed glumly. "Helyn and I each write them from the same address, and neither mentions the other. The last thing that they knew about us was that Helyn was a little bit queer, and that I was dead. Now they'll never believe us!"

Then his face suddenly brightened.

"Son," he exclaimed, seizing Larry by the arm, "why didn't I think of it before! There is one man in the whole world, who knows that I am alive, that Helyn is sane, that the new-soul menace is real. A man of unquestioned standing and veracity."

"Who?"

"Sir Francis Maxon!"

The next morning, as luck would have it, Blackstone Kent was sent to the railroad station on camp business, and was able to get off the following unsigned cable to Sir Francis, at his London address:

> Golf. Bretton Woods and Oakley. Have British Ambassador communicate with Attorney General that I am sane and my information to District Attorney Boston authentic.

He took his life in his hands, in sending it; but the risk was necessary.

DR. CHAPIN and Aaron Cohen were engaged in earnest conversation in the latter's office in the Administration Building. Strange to relate, they were discussing not dreams of empire, but rather—women.

"As soon as I am Emperor of America," Cohen said coolly, "I am going to have you operate on Helyn Kent and remove her moth-grub soul. I have kept my hands off her, because I plan to marry her in state in the White House. But, being human myself, I want a human bride."

"I think you are making a mistake," asserted the young doctor. "I prefer 'em Whoomangs. As I have repeatedly tried to impress on you, it makes 'em more docile."

"You would like them as Whoomangs," replied Cohen, "for you're a Whoomang yourself. Like mates with like."

"Is that so?" asked Dr. Chapin enigmatically. "It strikes me that Helyn is almost human, as is. The insertion of a moth-grub soul doesn't ruin any one with a real strong character. Take, for example, Quivven, and Eliot Endicott, and myself; we're quite human in spite of being Whoomangs. Dr. Ronk and Swami Singh are almost untouched by the operation. And even this little head nurse whom I have for a mistress; why, damn it, man, she's too darn human, as it is! Likely to scratch out my eyes, if I so much as look at another woman."

The doctor paused for a moment and reflected. Then continued, "Say, Aaron, do me a favor. Ship this nurse to another camp by the wireless matter-transmitter, will you, like a good fellow? I'm fed up with her. I've got another little cutie picked out for myself. Saw her to-day in the hospital here. A blond baby-doll with blue eyes."

Cohen shrugged but agreed, and went at once to the electrical laboratory. On arrival he told his two personal attendants, Red and Boris, to go to the hospital, and bring him the head nurse. Then he had the matter-transmitting apparatus overhauled, and got in touch with one of their camps in Mexico. By the time that the girl entered, accompanied by the two guards, all was in readiness, and the head electrician, Dr. Polakowski, was standing at the switch-panel.

The nurse arrived, all unsuspecting. But she was not left long in doubt as to why she had been sent for.

"You are being transferred to Las Rosas," announced Cohen briefly. "Step into the cubicle, please."

"Of course, Victor is going there, too?" she asked.

"Unfortunately Dr. Chapin remains here," replied Cohen tersely.

"Then I shall remain here," she defiantly declared.

"What!" exclaimed Cohen. "Why, young lady, remember that you are Whoomang."

"I'm also a woman," she retorted, "and Victor belongs to me."

"I rather thought," answered Cohen dryly, "that it was you who belonged to him. He's through with you, and now you are going to go to Las Rosas like a loyal little Whoomang."

"I refuse!" she exclaimed, stamping her foot.

"Think carefully," said Cohen, levelly. "This is treason. The penalty for treason is death. We shall not send you to Las Rosas against your will. We shall merely hold your body so that your head alone lies inside the coördinate axes. Then when Polakowski closes the switch, your head will be in Las Rosas, and your body here. Very simple and painless. Do you still refuse to have the *whole* of you transmitted to Las Rosas?"

"I still refuse," she said, quietly.

"Seize her, men," ordered Cohen.

In an instant, she was in the grasp of Red and Boris, who carried her, struggling, to the cubicle, and laid her head just across the threshold. Cohen gave a signal to Dr. Polakowski.

"Stand by to receive," spoke the electrician into the transmitter.

"All ready," replied his earphones faintly, with a strong Spanish accent.

"Stop! Stop!" screamed the now terrified girl, "I have valuable information for the organization. About treachery! Let me trade it for my life."

"Hold up, Polakowski," commanded Cohen. Then to the nurse, "Well, what is it?"

THE GUARDS still held her down. Incoherently she babbled out the tale of what she had seen and heard through the keyhole of Dr. Chapin's office, when Quivven the Goldenflame had bought, with a kiss, immunity for Eliot Endicott. Also the nurse recounted having heard Chapin, a little bit later, confess to Endicott that he (Chapin) had no new-soul. Also she told of the operation on Endicott, in which she had assisted, and in which the moth-grub had been intentionally omitted.

Cohen listened, with the smile of a forming purpose gradually spreading over his face.

"Is that all?" he asked.

"Yes," she replied. "And now I guess you will want to save me to testify against him."

"You guess wrong, double crosser," asserted Cohen. "Proceed, Polakowski."

"Stand by to receive," spoke the latter.

"All ready," replied his earphones.

For a moment, the little nurse remained stricken dumb with surprise. Then she let out a fearful shriek. But the shriek changed to a gurgle, as Polokowski threw the switch, and a fountain of blood poured from the headless neck of his victim.

"She won't bother her dear Victor any more," remarked Cohen dryly.

"What's the reason for that, if I may ask?" Polakowski inquired.

"You may not," snapped Cohen. "Here, you two hunkies: clean up the mess."

A chatter of startled inquiries came over the earphones from Las Rosas where a cleanly severed head had fallen to the floor of the cubicle. As Cohen strode out of the laboratory, Dr. Polakowski was busily explaining to their Mexican headquarters that the wages of treason is death.

Direct to the hospital went Cohen, and rapped on the door of Dr. Chapin's office.

"Come in," said a male voice.

Cohen entered. Chapin was seated in a chair, with his latest fancy, the blue-eyed blonde, in his arms.

"Your chief nurse has just been executed for treason," reported Cohen.

The doctor raised his eyebrows slightly, then remarked to the girl in his lap, "You see, my dear, that it doesn't pay to get jealous."

"I should worry," replied his latest. "If you quit loving me, I'll get me another boy-friend. But I'll be true to you, as long as you are to me. Is that O.K.?"

"It's disgusting!" interjected Cohen. "Send her away, Chapin. I want to talk to you."

"Toddle along, baby," said the doctor, and the new nurse obediently withdrew.

"On second thought," announced Cohen, "let's talk outside. Some one might be listening."

So the two of them stepped out into the open, and Cohen continued, "Some one did listen, Victor, that time that Quivven kissed you in your office."

Chapin turned pale.

His accuser went on, "And that same person listened when you confessed to Eliot Endicott that you have no new-soul. And that same person assisted at the operation in which you intentionally omitted to insert a moth-grub in Eliot Endicott's brain."

BY THIS time the doctor had recovered his poise.

Smiling maliciously, he countered with, "And that same person has just been executed for treason. Of course, Aaron, her stories were mere lies, thought up because of her insane jealousy. But, even supposing they had been true, she's dead now; how can you prove it?"

"Three other witnesses to her statement, besides myself," asserted Cohen.

"Mere hearsay, as against my denial."

"Not mere hearsay," corrected Cohen. "but rather a statement *in extremis*, that is to say, on the eve of death."

"That may be a principle of law," replied the doctor calmly. "I'm no lawyer, so I don't know. But I venture that the triumvirate would take my say so on all this, as against mere hearsay. They'd believe me, a Whoomang, against a soulless human such as you. Especially with Quivven to back me up."

That was so. Aaron Cohen suddenly realized that his accusation implicated one of the triumvirate, as well as Victor Chapin. But he was stunned for only a moment. Then he smiled, and the doctor knew from the smile that Aaron had the upper hand.

Said Aaron, "Swami Singh can make you tell the truth."

Chapin started. Then he said noncommittally, "What do you want, anyway?"

"I want you to suspect that Helyn is not a Whoomang. Operate on her for the ostensible purpose of finding out, and of inserting another new-soul, if anything should turn out to have happened to her original one; but actually to remove the one that is ready there."

Chapin whistled.

"This is getting sufficiently complicated," said he. "All right, I'll do it. And now let me tell you something. I'll bet you a good cigar that Helyn has no moth-grub soul right now. I'm a doctor, and have been observing her rather closely for some time. I've been saving up the information for some time when it might come in handy."

Aaron Cohen looked startled. But he was destined to be even more startled in a moment, for Red and Boris came rapidly around the corner of the building, and seized the two conferees by the scuff of the neck.

"What does this mean?" shouted Cohen. "I'll have you whipped for this outrage!"

Then, with that mixture of truculence and servility which so often characterizes a servant who has at last got the upper hand over his master, Red replied, grinning, "You've been rough to me for the last time, mister. As you said yourself to the nurse 'The wages of treason is death.'"

CHAPTER XVII

DESPERATE MEASURES

ARON COHEN AND Dr. Victory Chapin were unceremoniously dragged into the presence of the dread triumvirate. Helyn was there, also under arrest. To the doctor's relief, it soon developed that he was wanted merely as a witness. The accusation of treason was against Cohen alone.

One of Helyn's letters to the authorities had been intercepted. Spies had immediately been planted on the U.S. Attorney at Boston, and he reported that he took no stock in her letters, believing her to be unbalanced. In fact, her insanity was believed hereditary; her father had suffered from hallucinations too, and had probably jumped overboard.

No harm had been done to the cause by her letters, but she must be disciplined. Swami Singh had already examined her, under the influence of his hypnotic powers, and thus they had complete record of her treason. Also they now knew that her new-soul had been removed by Sir Francis Moxon, and that the reporter Lawrence Larrabee was lurking as a spy in their very midst.

Quivven confirmed this; she had tumbled upon Helyn in the act of kissing one of the guards. Helyn knew nothing of her father's presence, and accordingly she had reported to Swami Singh that her father's death had been genuine.

"Her perfidy is a most fortunate occurrence," boomed forth the huge ant through his radio speech-apparatus. "Now all we have to do is to identify this Larrabee person, and the great

Day can dawn without opposition. What fools these Americans are, to disregard her clear warning!"

Then the Great Three accused Cohen of knowing that his sweetheart was no longer a Whoomang.

He vehemently denied the accusation, and then added, "But even if it were true, is there not more justice in my having a human mate than in Quivven's doing so? For I am permitted, by the compact, to remain human, whereas Quivven is a Whoomang."

"Stop!" shouted the golden princess. "What do you mean? Eliot Endicott is one of us."

"Ask Chapin here," demanded Cohen unabashed. "I have full proof that Chapin is not a Whoomang himself, and that he left out the moth-grub, when he operated on Eliot Endicott. He did it at the express request of the Goldenflame."

"It's a lie!" shouted Dr. Chapin and Quivven in unison.

Meanwhile an attendant had been jotting down the proceedings in Porovian shorthand, for the benefit of the big gray dragon. The dragon now wrote something with a stylus held in one wing-claw, and handed the paper to Doggo.

The antman announced, "All humans, or even suspected humans, are under arrest, by the order of the King. This includes Cohen, Chapin, Helyn Kent, Eliot Endicott—"

"Not my Eliot!" shouted Quivven. "I'll vouch personally for him. I demand his freedom as a right."

More conference in shorthand between the ant and the dragon.

Then, "All right. The King will release Eliot Endicott on the personal recognizance of the Princess. Boris, take Dr. Chapin to Swami Singh for cross-examination under hypnosis. One of you other attendants, send for Sergeant Stone."

A few minutes later Blackstone Kent, having just returned from town, was ushered into the presence of the triumvirate. The lawyer saw with horror that Helyn and Cohen were under arrest, and instantly he sensed that there was all kinds of trouble in the air; but his face remained expressionless.

"Sergeant," announced the ant, "all humans must be rounded up at once. This girl here is not one of us. She has been giving out information. She has been kissing one of your guards. She has told Swami Singh that this guard is a human and is named Lawrence Larrabee. Line up the whole guard for inspection, and march them to the psychological laboratory. Singh will put the girl under the influence again, and will make her identify the spy."

Helyn slumped to the floor, and began to sob. Her father flashed her one glance, but dared not reveal the love and compassion which he felt for her.

Woodenly he inquired, "When do you wish them, your majesty?"

"Line them up at once. We shall phone the guard barracks when we are ready for them."

"Very well, your highness. It shall be done."

And Blackstone Kent, alias Sergeant Stone of the Whoomangs, withdrew.

UPON reaching the guard quarters, he sent one of the men along the fence to round up the sentries and bring them in. Then, merely telling him "There's hell to pay," he dispatched Larry to the barracks of the new employees, to dismiss all the guards there, and take charge himself.

As soon as all his men, except Larry, had reported and had turned in their automatics. Kent formed them in two ranks and put them under one of the corporals.

"At ease!" he commanded. "Await orders."

A few minutes later, in response to telephonic orders, he directed them to report to Swami Singh. As soon as they had departed, Kent made a beeline for the quarters of the new employees—the men who had arrived that day and the day before, and had not yet been operated upon. There were nearly a hundred of them.

Gathering them quickly in one end of their bunk house, Kent asked, "How many of you have had military service?"

All but a few of the younger men, held up their hands, for of late the Whoomangs had been specializing in recruiting ex-service men, so as to save the necessity of drilling or training them for the great drive.

"Good!" exclaimed Kent.

And then he embarked upon the greatest speech of his career. He had been noted for his oratory; yet never before in his impassioned addresses to juries, with the lives of clients at stake, had he waxed as eloquent as he did this day; for to-day it was not one life at stake, but millions, the lives or freedom of all the citizens of the United States.

He told his audience that they had been hired by a band of criminals, to assist in overthrowing the government of the United States, and to place an emperor in the White House. He sketched to them, in all its gruesome details, the system of moth-grub new-souls. He appealed to their gratitude for his saving them from this fate, to their instinct of self-preservation, and to their patriotism.

When he finished his harangue, the men arose with a cheer, and agreed to follow wherever Kent might lead.

Blackstone Kent then lined them up according to former rank. There were, among them, four ex-officers of the World War, and one ex-sergeant of the regular Army. In less time than it takes to tell, they had piled out of the barracks, had formed ranks, and the highest ranking ex-officer, standing in front of them, had gravely saluted Kent, and reported, "Sir, the company is formed."

Kent returned the salute.

"Follow me," he commanded, and strode toward the guard house, with Larry at his side.

"Right by squads—march!" snapped the captain, and the company swung into column of squads in their wake.

"But what's it all about?" asked Larry, bewildered.

So Kent told him of Helyn's arrest, and her confession under hypnosis. Now was the time to strike for freedom and victory, if ever.

At the guard house, the automatics and forty-five caliber ammunition of the dismissed Whoomang guardsmen were handed out as far as they would go. Then Kent marched his men toward the storehouses, where were kept all the rifles and rifle-ammunition, supplies more than sufficient to arm the entire camp, and to render them invincible against Kent's mere handful, unless Kent got there first.

The cheer, with which Kent's audience had greeted the conclusion of his remarks, had been a great mistake. It had been heard and interpreted at various points throughout the camp.

The quickest mind to grasp its full significance had been that of Aaron Cohen. Aaron, under arrest for treason to the cause.

"Let me go!" he begged of Doggo. "I'll bet that that Larrabee person has roused the new employees, while all the guards, except himself are up being identified by Helyn Kent. What a risk we're taking! Let me go, or our dreams of empire are at an end."

The huge ant had brains enough to take a chance.

"Release him," he thundered, and the next moment Aaron Cohen was racing toward Rajindra Singh's laboratory.

THERE in front of the laboratory stood the guardsmen, spread out in a semicircle, with Helyn in the center, seated in a chair, and the Swami standing by her, with one hand on her head.

"Who's in command?" shouted Cohen, breaking in unceremoniously upon the séance.

"I am," reported a corporal.

"Rush your men to storehouse 13," ordered Cohen. "Smash the doors, and arm your men. Your own quarters and pistols have already been captured. As soon as you're through at the storehouse, rouse the camp, issue arms to all Whoomangs, and send a small body of men to guard the triumvirate. Now, beat it! Don't wait to form ranks. Run!"

Then, as the guardsmen hurried pell-mell toward the store-house, he turned to Rajindra Singh and directed him to bring Helyn out of her trance, and take her at once to the administration building. He himself wasted no time on Helyn, for she was unconscious. Love must wait on empire.

Then he entered the laboratory. Dr. Chapin, bound and guarded by two thugs, stood inside.

Cohen glared triumphantly at the doctor.

"I rather think, Victor," he announced, "that I shall have to kill you. Quivven will appreciate your removal. And with you gone, I believe that I can trade Eliot Endicott's safety for Helyn's. Your continued existence complicates matters. Here, guard, give me your revolver."

He was accustomed to receive unquestioning obedience from these Whoomangs, but the two guards both raised their weapons menacingly.

"No, you don't, Mr. Cohen," snarled one of them. "You've been arrested as a human. We don't obey you any more."

Aaron started to argue, but Dr. Chapin cut in with, "Don't take any chances, men. Carry out the orders of your ruler, Doggo, which were to guard me carefully. Mr. Cohen has escaped from arrest. You'd better round him up, too."

While they were making up their minds, Cohen hurried out of gunshot, and ran toward the storehouse, where fighting was already in progress.

The entire unarmed Whoomang guard, that had been at Rajindra Singh's, had reached the storehouse just ahead of Kent's loyal Americans, and had battered in the door and secured rifles. But the Americans, nothing daunted, had charged with a cheer into the very teeth of the rifle-fire, and were now fighting it out hand-to-hand within the building. Those of them who were unarmed, had seized rifles at the first opportunity, and were now holding the doorway of the storehouse against the arriving hordes of unarmed Whoomangs.

In the fighting inside, Kent's men, being for the most part

armed with short-range weapons, had the advantage, and soon succeeded in killing or driving out the enemy. But unfortunately the enemy carried with them, in their retreat, quite a number of rifles; and soon began to snipe back from a distance at Kent's forces, who at once took cover in and around the building.

Blackstone Kent then counted up his losses: twenty-one dead or seriously wounded, to at least thirty-three of the Whoomangs. And Larry was nowhere to be found.

"A few more such victories, and I am undone," he quoted sadly.

But he had seventy-five fully armed and enthusiastic soldiers. Loading each soldier with all the ammunition that the man could carry, and making sure that each had one rifle, but no, more, he set fire to the storehouse and evacuated.

Then began the advance toward the administration building, whither all the unarmed Whoomangs had by now fled. Aaron Cohen remained on the firing line of his men, taking command of them, and fearlessly exposing himself whenever necessary.

At the first opportunity, he armed himself from the body of a dead Whoomang, but fortunately for Victor Chapin, the battle had by this time passed beyond the building in which the doctor was confined, and Chapin and his two captors were now prisoners of Kent's Americans.

CHAPTER XVIII

AN EXPENSIVE VICTORY

BOTH SIDES WERE keeping carefully under cover, each side potting any member of the other who exposed himself. The armed BWhoomangs, being greatly outnumbered by the Americans, were steadily forced backward. The thousand or so unarmed Whoomangs had already retreated to the administration building.

Then Cohen remembered the death-ray. He cursed himself for having forgotten it. But, even so, victory was in his grasp once more. Turning over the command to a subordinate, he raced to the administration building, only to find that every one there had adjourned to the electrical laboratory. Well, that was even better, for that was where the death-ray machine was located.

He reached the laboratory, commandeered some men, hauled out the machine, and set it up in front of the building. The electrical connections were all plainly labeled, so that it was an easy matter to wire it up to terminals inside the laboratory.

Now let the Americans come! Aaron Cohen could stand off thousands of them, and there were only sixty or seventy of them to stand off.

But he himself did not know how to run the death-dealing apparatus. So he sent one of his men inside for Dr. Polakowski.

The robot returned and reported that the electrician was busy at the matter-transmitting apparatus, and that the King would not permit him to leave.

Cursing, Aaron told the man to find some one else inside, who understood the machine; and presently to his intense relief the messenger returned with an unusually intelligent-looking young man, a workman or guardsman, to judge from his wearing overalls instead of the smock of a laboratory worker or the white coat of a doctor or interne. In fact, he was clearly a guardsman, and not a mere worker, for he was armed with an automatic.

"**CAN YOU** run this?" demanded Cohen.

"Bet your life," replied the young man. "Dr. Polakowski has thoroughly explained it to me. I'm assigned to it, in case of war, sir!"

"Well, it's a case of war, right now," asserted Cohen. "Turn it on as soon as the Americans appear."

Then he sent one of his men to order all his troops to retreat precipitately.

"When the Americans see the retreat and charge us," he exalted, rubbing his hands, "then good night for them. Why, even if they don't charge, this ray will sweep through ground and buildings, and all other cover, and demolish the enemy. In a few minutes, the world will be safe for the Whoomangs."

Presently his own battle-line came piling back on him. A few minutes later, the charging Americans appeared.

"Let 'em have it!" shouted Cohen.

The guardsman promptly manipulated the apparatus, but nothing happened to the party of oncoming Americans.

With a curse, Cohen struck the guardsman over the head with the butt of his automatic, spilling him unconscious to the ground; then rushed to the matter-transmitting apparatus and dragged Dr. Polakowski unceremoniously from his switch-panel.

"Quick!" shouted Cohen. "The death-ray! The fate of the empire is at stake!"

Polakowski reached the machine in time. The oncoming forces of Kent, fearing some sort of ambush, had taken to cover once more, just short of reaching the building.

Expertly the electrician seized the levers of the death-ray machine, handling them in quite a different way than that in which the young guardsman had been manipulating them.

"Let 'em have it!" shouted Cohen jubilantly. "Their cover won't protect them now."

But Dr. Polakowski let out a groan of dismay.

"Sabotage!" he exclaimed. "Some one has wrecked it."

Then shots from the attacking Americans drove them both into the building.

Polakowski returned at once to his former post at the switches of the matter-transmitting apparatus; where, under orders from the King, he had been evacuating the camp. Quivven and her consort were gone. Doggo was gone. Gone was every animal, and every male Whoomang except those who were armed, those who had not fled to this building, and one or two others.

As Cohen followed Polakowski into the room, all that were left there were the gray dragon, Helyn Kent, four men, and the electrician himself.

The dragon was seated in the cubicle, and one of the men was just about to close the curtains. Polakowski was at the levers. The dragon, seeing Cohen enter, clicked three times. It was the signal for paper and stylus. A man brought it. The dragon pressed the paper to the floor with one wing-claw, and wrote rapidly with the other.

"Give *me* some paper," shouted Cohen. "I want to report to the King before he scuttles off and leaves us."

So paper was given to Cohen, too, but before he finished, the dragon's communication had been handed up to Polakowski.

The Pole read a few lines, and then directed, "Seize Cohen."

Two of the men were holding Helyn. The other two promptly jumped for Aaron, and disarmed him.

Then Dr. Polakowski continued, "This is what the King says. He trusts no humans any more. He will now leave, but I must not tell where. Helyn is to be sent first, however. After they have both gone, I am to send you, Cohen, to another location, where you will be kept in prison and later executed. Eliot Endicott is to be killed. Helyn Kent is to be killed, but first she is to be the plaything of the King himself."

A WAVE of revulsion swept over Cohen. This was gratitude for you! He had brought the triumvirate down from the Planet Venus. He had betrayed his country for his own mad ambition. He had been absolutely loyal to these masters from beyond the skies. He had just escaped from arrest at their hands, to lead an almost successful plan to save them, while they had done nothing except scuttle away. And now his reward at their hands was not trust and honor, but rather torture and death! Worse than that, torture and death for the girl he loved!

All during the growth of the organization, Aaron Cohen must have been insane, blinded by delusions of grandeur, and dreams of empire. Now it was all swept from him by the perfidy and ingratitude of the three beasts from another world, whom he had served so faithfully. Now he became suddenly sane, coldly and clearly sane.

After all, he was an American, too! Was there nothing that he could do to atone for his treason to the country of his birth? Was there nothing that he could do to save Helyn from this ghastly fate?

His agile and brilliant mind raced over all the possibilities. It would do no good to struggle against the two Whoomang thugs who were holding him. He must think, and think hard!

Meanwhile Helyn and her two captors stepped into the cubicle. She smiled bravely at Aaron. Never had he loved her so deeply as at this moment. And she herself was not unmoved by his downfall. True, she did not love him, but he had always been kind to her, and had treated her with gentlemanly respect; so now she pitied him from the bottom of her heart, pitied him even more than she did herself. In fact, she had such an abiding faith in the justice of her cause, that she felt certain that the threats of King Boomalayla against her would never be carried into effect.

"Good-by, Aaron," she called. "Forgive me."

"Good-by, Helyn," he replied. "Always remember that I loved you."

Then the curtains were drawn, the formula repeated at the switchboard, and the switches were closed. When one of Aaron's guards stepped forward and pulled the curtains open again, the cubicle was empty.

Boomalayla now waddled onto the platform.

"Tuck in his wings carefully," cautioned Dr. Polakowski. "He is such an irregular shape, I am always fearful that some of him will get left behind."

The guard drew the curtains, and made careful inspection for projecting portions of the King's anatomy.

"O.K.," he reported, stepping back from the curtains.

"Stand by to receive," droned Dr. Polakowski.

"All ready," replied his earphones.

So he threw the switches.

But at just that instant, Aaron Cohen wrenched himself free from the single guard who still had him, and dived at the curtains.

His move had been well-timed.

When Dr. Polakowski opened the switches again, Cohen's waist and hips and legs lay against the curtain of one side of the cubicle, smearing it with blood. The rest of his body was gone. There was a large hole in the curtain, where it had been pushed into the influence of the coordinate axes.

On the farther side of the cubicle, the curtain bellied out.

Frantically the two guards tore open the front hangings, exposing the interior to view. Piled against the bellied-out curtain was a bloody heap of pieces of dragon, including a still-blinking severed head.

Thus Aaron Cohen atoned.

FROM the receiving station, which had just been showered with fragments of Cohen and the King, was coming a frantic babbling of inquiries, but Dr. Polakowski cut them short with, "Stand by to receive."

Then he ordered the two men, "Jump to it!"

But, Whoomangs though they were, they shook their heads and shied away from the gory cubicle. Then Blackstone Kent burst into the room at the head of his decimated but victorious troops.

One of the guards fired, and was promptly shot down. The other dropped his automatic, and surrendered. The Americans crowded into the room. Several of them entered the cubicle to examine the dismembered wreckage of the dragon. Dr. Polakowski was still at the switch-panel. With a diabolical grin, he closed two switches.

But Blackstone Kent, just an instant before, had sensed the danger.

"'Ten-shun!" he shouted.

The habits of their Army days were strong, even after all these years. Instantly every man clicked his heels together, and stood erect.

Just in time, too! The cubicle became a cube of pearly fire, and the men within it vanished from sight. A moment before, some part of practically every one of them had been across the dividing-line.

"Stand away from that switch-panel!" bellowed Kent.

In his mind there suddenly formed a purpose to follow, through space, the men who had vanished, and thus take the war into the enemy's territory, as it were. At the other end, they could drive the enemy away from the matter-transmitting apparatus, which they themselves would hold, and thus they could prevent a repetition of the wholesale escape which had taken place here.

But even as Dr. Polakowski stepped away from the panel, in seeming obedience to Kent's order, he closed another switch. A sheet of flame shot across the face of the panel, and it crumbled; and, at the same instant, the three coordinate axes within the cubicle crashed together in a twisted heap.

"You see," remarked Dr. Polakowski dryly, as though addressing a classroom full of students, "we are prepared for any emergency, even defeat. King Boomalavla is dead, but Doggo and Quivven will carry on. The king is dead, long live the king! And now, gentlemen, I surrender."

"Never mind the heroics," snapped Kent. "To what headquarters have they all gone?"

"That," replied their captive coolly, "you can't make me tell. No amount of torture, no threat of death, can make a Pole disloyal."

"Perhaps not," countered Kent. "But you will change your allegiance, when we remove that little squirming worm from the base of your brain."

"I rather think not," asserted Polakowski, smiling, "for I have just taken poison."

Then, with the smile of triumph still on his face, he suddenly slumped to the floor and lay still.

Kent was in a grim quandary. Victory was snatched from his very grasp, with Helyn gone, Jack Blakeslee and Lawrence Larrabee missing. Two of the triumvirate had escaped! He believed Cohen, too, had escaped, for how could he know that the mangled remains were those of his recent antagonist?

What had he to show for his great battle, except one dead dragon?

And the day which had been set for the overthrow of America was less than a week off!

CHAPTER XIX

OFFICIAL INCREDULITY

AT LEAST, KENT could consolidate his captured ground.

He had fifty of his American fighters left. The prisoners numbered about a hundred, including guardsmen, nurses, a few assorted laborers who hadn't reached the electrical laboratory, and Dr. Victor Chapin.

The doctor was full of gratitude for having been saved from the wrath of Aaron Cohen; and furthermore he was still loyal to the one cause which had always claimed his allegiance, namely, the filling of his own pocketbook. So he at once offered his services to the conqueror.

"You can trust me," he insisted. "Can't you see that I was under arrest by your enemy? Besides, I'm not a Whoomang, and never was. That's what they arrested me for, when they found it out."

"I trust you just about as far as you could throw a bull by the tail," asserted Kent, grimly. "But perhaps you can be useful. Have you any suggestions?"

"Yes," replied Dr. Chapin, eagerly. "Don't trust a single Whoomang. Give me about four of your most agile-fingered men to help me, and I'll start taking the moth-grubs out of the nurses. As soon as the nurses convalesce, I can use them, and give you back the men you've loaned me. Then we can start operating on the male Whoomangs. Only—may I keep Alice a Whoomang?"

"And who is Alice?"

"My latest girl. Being a Whoomang makes 'em more docile."

"On the contrary," replied Kent, "I think you had better *start* with Alice. If you intend to work yourself into my good graces, you had better not have a pretty little Whoomang hanging round you."

So Kent gave orders to release Chapin; but for one of the corporals, armed, to remain constantly with him. Then the male Whoomangs were herded into one barracks, and the females into another. Squads of prisoners, under guard, were set to work collecting the dead and wounded. The Whoamang dead, recognizable by their scars, were piled in one place, and the humans in another. Dr. Chapin, assisted by a couple of nurses under guard, tested each alleged corpse for signs of life.

The wounded were carried to the hospital, and given first aid. Among them, to Kent's great surprise were found Lawrence Larrabee, merely stunned, and Eliot Endicott, severely wounded.

Eliot had fought loyally for his Quivven, defending the laboratory, so that she might escape. His body was riddled by American bullets, and his life was despaired of.

Larry, during the fight for control of the munitions storehouse, had suddenly thought of the death-ray and the matter-transmitter, and accordingly had rushed to the power-house, with the idea of cutting off the power, and thus depriving the enemy of means for either fighting or escaping. Finding the power-house too well guarded, he had gone to the laboratory, where he had arrived just in time to volunteer to operate the death-ray machine for Aaron Cohen. As soon as he had got his hands on the apparatus, he had pulled loose a number of wires. Then Aaron had struck at him with a revolver butt, and Larry had known no more, until he came to his senses again in the hospital.

Among the dead, there was the lower half of a human body. Dr. Chapin at once, and with great glee, identified it as a part of Aaron Cohen.

"I recognized the suit which he was wearing!" exclaimed the

doctor. "Well, he won't be crowned Emperor of America five days from now!"

For a moment, Kent was jubilant. Then his face sobered.

"I know exactly what the organization will do," he asserted. "At least, it's what I would do in their place; and it's so obviously the proper move, since they no longer have to fulfill their pledge to Cohen, that I don't see how they can overlook it. From their point of view, it will be a decided improvement on their original plan, and a lot harder for us to cope with."

"What is it?" asked Chapin, much interested.

"I'd rather not tell you," replied Blackstone Kent.

THE PLAN which Kent feared was this: Two of the President's Cabinet were said to be Whoomangs. Therefore all that the organization would have to do would be to assassinate the President, the Vice President, Secretary of State, Secretary of the Treasury, and so on down until they came under the presidential succession law, to a Cabinet member who was a Whoomang.

Thus a Whoomang would become President of the United States in a perfectly constitutional manner and would have until March 4, 1933, to consolidate his position. By that time, with his aid, the organization could have made themselves absolutely invincible.

It was too diabolically simple. It was undoubtedly what the brains of Doggo and Quivven would plan. They would probably still hold to the original date set for the *coup d' état*, changing only this one feature of the plan.

This left Blackstone Kent just five days in which to block them. His plans were formed in an instant.

The World War captain who had so ably led the handful of Kent's Americans to victory that day, was placed in command of the camp, with instructions to guard the Whoomang prisoners, both male and female, and see that they were all restored to a human state as rapidly as possible.

There were plenty of supplies, and so there was no need of

any communication with the outside world. Dr. Chapin was adjured to take the best possible care of Eliot Endicott, who was by now delirious.

From Chapin, Kent obtained as complete a list as the doctor could remember, of the cities and street addresses of the various establishments of the organization. But unfortunately the information as to the key location, namely the one in Washington, D.C., was extremely meager.

"You see, it is not a camp, and has no hospital," Chapin explained, "and so we didn't go there on our recent nation-wide tour of inspection. There's nothing in Washington, but a large vacant storehouse, four death-ray machines, a matter-transmitter, and a few guards. I haven't the slightest idea as to what part of the city the building is located in, as our Washington establishment has been moved recently."

Nor could Kent and he find any information on the subject among the papers at the administration building. Nor did any of these papers, which had been most subtly kept, contain anything incriminating for Kent to show the authorities.

Kent then set out for Washington, to make one last frantic appeal to the Attorney-General. Now that he had found the missing assistant district attorney, Kent felt that the authorities *must* listen. Then, too, Sir Francis Moxon might by this time have received Kent's cablegram, and have communicated with the British ambassador.

But how to prove to the authorities that Eliot Endicott had actually been found? True, the department could send an operative to this Wisconsin north woods camp; but, by the time the operative had made his inspection and had reported, the day set by the organization for their seizure of the government would have come and gone.

Suddenly Blackstone Kent had an inspiration. Getting a rubber-stamp, ink-pad from the administration building, he made several sets of fingerprints from the unconscious Endicott. Of course, there was a chance that Eliot had never had his finger-prints recorded, but if he ever had, and the two sets of prints were now compared, the authorities would have to believe Kent's story, or at least a part of it.

Larry begged to be taken to Washington, and was so eager to do what he could to locate and rescue Helyn, that Kent finally yielded, though the reporter had by no means recovered from the blow on his skull.

There was plenty of money in the safe in the administration building. Kent had the safe demolished with sledge-hammers, helped himself, and turned the rest over to the captain. Then one of his men drove him and Larry to the railroad.

The best that they could do was to flag a night freight for Duluth. From Duluth early the next morning they took a day-train for the twin cities, where they arrived just in time to change from overalls, their Whoomang uniform, into ready-made clothes, and catch the mail-plane for Milwaukee.

The great Day of the Whoomangs was only four days off.

IT WAS while they were winging their way from Minnesota to Milwaukee that Kent suddenly realized that they were putting all their eggs in one basket. Larry and he were the only persons in America who combined both the knowledge and the determination to combat the menace. What if one of the successive planes carrying them to Washington should crash and kill them both? So when they landed at the Milwaukee County airport, Kent insisted that the reporter travel the rest of the way by train.

And now it came in most handy that they had with them more than one set of Eliot Endicott's finger-prints. They divided the sets between them.

Then Larry took a taxi to town, while Kent boarded the Chicago night mail. At Chicago, Kent changed again for Washington, where he finally arrived the next morning.

The zero hour was now only *three* days off!

Blackstone Kent felt like Sheridan, "with Winchester twenty miles away."

From the Washington airport, he took a taxi to a hotel. Eager as he was to get started on his work, and much as he realized that every minute counted, yet he also realized that the entire success of his trip might depend upon the first impression which he created upon the officials. Accordingly he bathed, and shaved, and had his suit pressed. While waiting for the suit, he breakfasted in his room.

Then he made a bee-line for the British Embassy. To his surprise he was admitted at once.

"So you are Blackstone Kent?" asked the ambassador, with an amused smile on his lips. "Pray tell me what this pother is all about. My old friend, Sir Francis Moxon, wired me to tell the American Attorney-General that you were sane, and all that; but, my dear chap, that's an awful responsibility for His Britannic Majesty's government to take in a matter about which we know nothing at all."

"Sir," replied Kent, "there is a band of criminal master minds in this country, who are planning to assassinate the President and a number of other high officials. My nephew, Eliot Endicott, who is connected with the Department of Justice, was on their trail, but they kidnapped him. I located the place where they had him confined, up in New Hampshire, and notified the department. But there were so many weird and preposterous features to the situation, including the kidnaping and mental metamorphosis of my own daughter by these same criminals, that the district attorney at Boston, who was in charge of the case, began to doubt my sanity."

The ambassador murmured some polite deprecation.

Blackstone Kent continued, "While operatives from the department were on their way to New Hampshire to rescue young Endicott, he was spirited away. The criminals soft-soaped the operatives—"

"Actually?" interjected the Britisher. "How uncouth!"

"No, no!" laughed Kent. "That's an Americanism and means 'to cozen or beguile, with honeyed words and actions.' Well, anyway, the detectives reported that the crooks were gentlemen, and that I was a bit balmy, as you would say. So I pretended to get drowned, and then in disguise enlisted with the criminals; while my daughter pretended to fall in love with their leader. Both of us have sent repeated warnings to the authorities, but these warnings have gone absolutely unheeded. Within three days, the President, Vice-President and most of the members of the Cabinet are to be assassinated."

"My dear man," expostulated the ambassador, "you must admit that it sounds unbelievable. I am quite willing to accept the statement of Sir Francis that you are sane; for who should know better than a great alienist such as he! But, even so, you might be mistaken as to your facts. What proof have you?"

"If I have found Eliot Endicott, after the entire Department of Justice has searched for him for months without success," countered Kent, "would that constitute proof?"

"It would go a long way toward substantiating your entire story," admitted the ambassador. "But have you found him? And are you sure that he will not be spirited away again, as you say he was that time before?"

"He has been rescued, and is under a competent guard," Kent replied. "Here are his finger-prints, to prove his identity."

"I am tentatively convinced, sir, pending the identification of the prints. Pray, be seated, while I telephone your Attorney-General. England will be glad to render this service to America."

SO SAYING, the ambassador withdrew. Presently he returned, with a queer glint in his eye, and announced: "Your Attorney-General says that he knows all about you, and that you are a crank. But I rather think I flattened him by mentioning the finger-prints. May I send them over to him by messenger? He is wiring Boston at once for Mr. Endicott's record prints."

Suddenly there flashed across Kent's mind the possibility that the Attorney General might be one of the two Cabinet members who had been made Whoomangs. But luckily Kent had two sets of finger-prints on his person, and two other sets were with Larry.

"You may have one set," he replied.

"Thank you," said the official. "Come back about three.... Now, I know how impatient you must be, but everything depends on making the right approach to the Attorney-General. It will be worth the delay. By the way, why not get Sir Francis over here?"

"From London?" exclaimed Kent. "There wouldn't be time."

"Oh, no," laughed the ambassador. "He is at this moment visiting Derrik Van Dyck in New York."

Blackstone Kent rushed back to his hotel, and called the Van Dycks on the long distance phone. Luckily, Sir Francis was there. Kent's message was brief, as he did not want to intrust too much information to the wires. But he succeeded in getting the surgeon to agree to take an airplane at once to the capital, without a moment's delay.

At three o'clock that afternoon, Blackstone Kent and Sir Francis Moxon met at the British Embassy. And the ambassador had good news for them. The Attorney-General had received from Boston a photographic reproduction of Eliot Endicott's record finger-prints, transmitted by telegraph, and they checked exactly with the sample brought by Kent. Accordingly, the Attorney-General would see them at once.

The three men went over to the Department of Justice together, and were shown immediately into the office of the Department chief.

As soon as they had all shaken hands, Kent asked, "Do you mind if I take a look at the back of your head?"

"What!" exclaimed the Attorney-General, with mingled surprise and amusement. "Is this a retaliation for the times when some members of our Department have suggested that *you* ought to have *your* head examined?"

"No," replied Kent, dryly. "It's merely a very necessary precaution."

CHAPTER XX

IN THE SHADOW OF DOOM

BLACKSTONE KENT LOOKED at the back of the head of the Attorney-General. The hair was a bit sparse, so he saw at a glance that there was no scar. He heaved a sigh of relief.

"Now," said Kent, "we can continue."

Then, drawing the three men into the center of the room, and looking furtively around for animal eaves-droppers, he recounted the entire history of the case, from the original mysterious disappearance of Eliot Endicott, down to date.

Before either the Attorney-General or the British ambassador had time to cast any embarrassing aspersions on Kent's sanity, Sir Francis Moxon quickly cut in with what he knew of the situation. His testimony as to the unquestioned sanity of Blackstone Kent, and as to the moth-grub which he himself had extracted from Helyn Kent's skull, was simple and convincing.

Yet still the Attorney-General was unconvinced.

Said he, "You two gentlemen are undoubtedly sincere. But such things as you mention are impossible. Our administration would be laughed out of office if the newspapers ever got hold of the story that we had seriously believed in the existence of such an organization of criminals as you have just described."

"And so," retorted Kent, "instead of being laughed out of office, you prefer to be put out by assassination. Is that it?"

"Not at all!" rejoined the Attorney-General, somewhat testily. "I shall place strong extra guards over the President, the Vice

President, and every member of the Cabinet, for the next few days."

"There! That's a lot better," Kent interjected.

"Don't interrupt," continued the official. "I was about to say that that was all I feel justified in doing under the circumstances."

"And I," asserted the British ambassador, "shall feel called upon to inform my government that you are making a grave mistake."

The American official's fear of ridicule thus took another turn. He was between two fires.

"What!" exclaimed he. "Do you believe all this rot?"

"I know Sir Francis Moxon personally," replied the Britisher simply.

The Attorney-General crooked up his mouth, and reflected for a moment; then said he, "Well, perhaps I'm crazy, instead of the three of you. I'm certainly outnumbered. Mr. Kent, if you can bring me any corroborative evidence to-morrow morning, I'll listen to you."

The three withdrew, rather disheartened. What corroborative evidence could they possibly produce?

Exhausted both physically and mentally, Blackstone Kent returned to his hotel room, and went promptly to bed.

THE NEXT thing that he knew, his telephone bell was ringing, and it was broad daylight. Sleepily, he took off the receiver.

"Gentleman to see you," said a voice.

"Send him right up," Kent replied mechanically; then, suddenly alert. "No. Wait a minute. What's his name?"

"Lawrence Larrabee," said the voice.

"Oh, fine!" ejaculated Kent, much relieved. "Send him up."

Here was some corroborative evidence—not that it was much help.

While Kent shaved, Larry recounted an uneventful trip, and

asked many questions, which Kent answered monosyllabically through his lather.

Then they breakfasted together in the grillroom.

At nine o'clock sharp, the two presented themselves at the Department of Justice, and were promptly admitted.

"Mr. Kent," exclaimed the Attorney-General, warmly shaking his hand, "after you had gone, I got to thinking over your story, and finally decided that it would do no harm to protect you, too, overnight. My operatives arrested a man who was trying to enter your door with a pass-key. And, Mr. Kent—would you believe it?—the prisoner has a scar at the base of his skull!"

"Well, why not?" replied Kent, unimpressed. "No one without such a scar would be likely to be hanging around my door at night. But excuse my rudeness. I have been so beaten down by your Department's unbelief, that it is difficult for me to get up any enthusiasm, when you suddenly discover a bit of evidence which points my way. But I certainly am grateful to you for protecting me."

"Mr. Kent," said the official, kindly, "I quite understand your feeling. And I am beginning to believe in the truth of your story, though, of course—"

Kent finished the sentence for him, "Though of course the situation can't be as serious as I claim. Mr. Attorney-General, here is some corroborative testimony. May I present Mr. Lawrence Larrabee?"

Larry at once launched into an account of the part which he had played in the adventures.

When he finished, the Attorney-General exclaimed, "Gentlemen, I'll take a chance, and back you. My mind tells me that your story is preposterous, but caution urges me not to risk the safety of America. I will risk some secret measures. Where do we start?"

"Thank God that somebody has at last seen the light!" said Kent fervently. "We have just today and to-morrow before the date set for the great drive. Day after to-morrow, the organization will strike, if we haven't prevented them in the meantime. The first thing to do is to guard all our high executives, as never before. The second thing to do is to find that store-house! Meanwhile have your prisoner removed to Walter Reed Hospital, and let Sir Francis Moxon operate on him at once."

The Attorney-General rang for his assistant, examined the back of his skull, much to that official's surprise, and then sent him to gather up some of his most able and trusted Secret Service operatives.

These, in turn, protesting emphatically, were examined for external evidence of Whoomang souls; and then, no scars having been found, they were dispatched in groups, to comb the city for storehouses, or buildings which even remotely resembled storehouses.

Each such building was to be searched for electrical apparatus, and every attendant of such buildings was to have the back of his head examined for scars. The following parting instructions were given:

"Every bit of strange electrical apparatus is to be reported immediately to me by phone, leaving all but one man of your group to guard the machinery. Every person with a scar is to be arrested summarily, and held incommunicado in a windowless cell. You are to ask permission to search each place, assuring the person in charge that this performance has nothing whatever to do with either the Volstead Act or the Internal Revenue. If permission is refused, or if the building seems deserted, surround the building and phone me without an instant's delay."

"Never mind what it's all about; the less you know, the less beans you are likely to spill. Now go. Divide the district up into blocks, and comb each block thoroughly. Stick together in groups. Don't stop until you find what we are after, or are recalled because some one else has found it."

ALL THAT day, Blackstone Kent and Larry remained at the Department of Justice. The guards about the high executives were strengthened even further, but those officials themselves were not notified of the danger. This was for the purpose of not alarming the President and Vice President, and for quite a different reason in the case of the Cabinet. The operatives who guarded the Cabinet members were specially instructed to report immediately if their wards had scars in the backs of their heads, or communicated with any individuals having such scars, or were seen talking to animal pets.

The British Embassy called for extra police protection, which was granted. Additional guards were placed around the Department of Justice itself, and its offices were closed to the public, all appointments being canceled.

An air of tension prevailed in the Department.

From time to time, the telephone would ring, and one of the squads would report that some warehouse had refused to submit to search. Immediately an assistant would be sent to procure a warrant, and there would be great excitement, until it developed that there was nothing of interest at that particular location, and that the disinclination to being searched had been due merely either to caution on the part of a timid employee of the owners of the building, or to the fact that the owners themselves were insisting on their constitutional rights.

From time to time, one of the squads would locate some strange bit of electrical machinery, and an expert requisitioned for the day from the Bureau of Standards—would be sent under guard in a taxicab, to investigate. But he never found anything which was strange to him, about any of the apparatus.

Along toward evening, the Attorney-General began to grow impatient.

Blackstone Kent forestalled what might have been some sarcastic remarks on the part of that official, by saying, "Now you can appreciate how the Boston district attorney felt, when his operatives found nothing at the Jones Lumber Camp. And yet you and I know that there had been plenty there to find, if they had only been in time. I was in time at the camp in the

Wisconsin woods, and look at what I found! Let us devoutly hope that we are not too late here in Washington."

This mollified the Attorney-General for a while.

But at last four thirty came, with no results yet. The squads were recalled for the night. Kent and Larrabee returned to their hotel. Only a single day and two nights now intervened before the enemy were destined to strike!

The two allies discussed the situation in low tones.

"Do you believe that their local headquarters is somewhere in the suburbs?" asked Larry. "Or that it is located in some building that is too small to be classed as a warehouse?"

"I doubt it," replied Kent. "The explanation of our failure is probably much more simple."

HE PAUSED for a moment, deep in thought. Then suddenly exclaimed, "I have it! Come on!"

"What is it?" asked Larry excitedly, as they put on their coats.

"No time to explain," replied Kent. "Come on!"

But a burly individual, just outside their door, stopped them.

"I'm very sorry, sir," said he, "but I have orders not to let you leave your room."

"Who are you, anyway?" asked Kent, exasperated, meanwhile motioning to Larry to return into the room.

The reporter did so and closed the door, leaving the two men standing just outside. In that way Larry would be able to phone or shout for help if Kent should get into trouble.

"I'm from the Department," replied the burly man, flashing a badge.

"Your badge means nothing to me," asserted Kent. "Let me see the back of your head."

"Say, what's this all about?" asked the man. "This is the third time today that I've had my head examined. Are you folks all mind-readers? Or phrenologists? Or what?"

"If the Department wanted you to know, they would have told you," countered Kent. "Come on, let's see your skull."

Just then a second burly man appeared down the corridor. Signaling to him, the guard submitted to examination. There was no scar. Nor was there any scar on the second guard.

"It's all right, Larry," shouted Kent. "Come on out."

Cautiously the reporter emerged.

Then Kent asked, "Will you two men take a chance, and go with me to the house of the Assistant Attorney-General, who is in charge of this affair?"

The two detectives looked questioningly at each other, then agreed.

So the four of them took a taxi. Luckily the official was at home. A brief conference ensued, at which they went rapidly through a list of buildings which the assistant checked on the map of the District of Columbia as having searched that day.

While they were all inside, their taximan was telephoning from a near-drug store.

After the conference, Kent and Larrabee and the Assistant Attorney-General and the two detectives drove to the home of the Superintendent of Public Buildings, and then with him drove to his office, where he supplied Kent with a list of all the government barns and storehouses, and a map on which they were marked. Kent had him describe briefly the occupancy and frequency of use of each of these buildings.

After this conference, only four men got into the cab. An address on the outskirts of the city was given.

The Assistant Attorney-General and the Superintendent of Public Buildings stood on the curb and shouted, "Good-by, Mr. Kent. Good-by, Mr. Larrabee. Good-by and good luck!"

And they were off.

By now it was quite dark. The cab threaded strange streets for many minutes, then rumbled across a long bridge. Finally they were in the country.

Headlights ahead blocked their way. Both cars came to a jolting stop. The driver of the taxi got out and started to curse.

Several men emerged from the other car and swore back at him.

Then suddenly, without warning, the taxi driver and the occupants of the other car wheeled, and thrust revolvers into the cab. A moment later the four occupants lay bound and gagged and blindfolded inside. For the taxi driver was a Whoomang!

CHAPTER XXI

THE BATTLE IN THE BARN

CURIOUS THINGS WERE taking place in a supposedly vacant barn belonging to the Rock Creek Park system, near the northern boundary of the District of Columbia. Under cover of darkness, five men arrived in a high-powered car. Furtively they unlocked the building. Up into the lofts they went, one of them carrying a large bundle. All of them had flash lights. Then one of them opened an upstairs outside door, facing away from the road. The man who did this reached through the door and hung something just outside.

Taking pitchforks, they shoveled away certain piles of hay in the loft, uncovering various bits of machinery swathed in dusty canvas.

First they hauled out some sectional masts, hoisted them up to the cupola, pushed them out onto the roof, and erected them in sockets at the two ends of the ridgepole. A lobster-pot aërial was then strung between the masts and a wire run down into the building. They also connected up some underground wires which ran to other antennæ, already up, concealed in the near-by woods.

Other machinery was dug out of the concealing hay: a gasoline motor-generator set, a string of incandescent light bulbs, a switch panel, and a curtained cubicle containing three coördinate axes of some strange pale iridescent metal. All these were set up, and properly wired together. The men worked with a precision born of long experience.

The motor-generator set was put in motion, the electric lights were turned on, and one of the five men stationed himself at the switch panel, put earphones on his head, and began to adjust the variable capacities and variable inductances to his satisfaction. He called several stations, and conversed with them in low, guarded tones.

Meanwhile his four companions were uncovering four diabolical-looking machines, part of which resembled searchlights, and were carrying them down to the main floor of the barn.

At last the man at the panel announced, "All adjusted for matter-transmission."

Back spoke his earphones, "Stand by to receive."

He closed certain switches. A strange glow came through the cracks of the curtained cubicle.

"All ready," he replied, and turned his attention to a dial on his panel.

The needle of the dial swung from a position marked "Off" to one marked "On." Then, after about four seconds, it swung back to "Off" again. Instantly the young man opened the switches on the panel.

The light of the cubicle died, the curtains parted, and a huge black ant, several feet in length, clattered out. One of the other men had meanwhile come up from downstairs, and now produced a complicated set of radio apparatus, which he strapped to the head and thorax of the huge beast. For, of course, the antman could not carry his radio set with him, as the matter-transmitter would not transmit metals.

When this apparatus had been properly adjusted and tuned, the antman boomed forth, "Who is in charge here?"

"I am, your highness," replied the young man at the switch panel.

"Your name?"

"John Blake, your highness."

"I shall remember it. You are handling things here very ef-

ficiently. After the Great Day has come, I shall see that you are
properly rewarded."

"Thank you, your highness."

"And now, where are the death-ray machines?"

"Downstairs, your highness, awaiting the arrival of the operators."

The huge ant lumbered down the stairs, accompanied by the
man who had helped him put on his radio set, while the youth
returned to his panels.

"Stand by to receive," spoke the earphones.

As before, he threw the switches and replied, "All ready."

When he restored his switches to neutral, Quivven the Goldenflame stepped from the curtains and glanced inquiringly
around.

INSTANTLY the young man closed another switch. A sheet
of ruddy fire spread across the panel, and it crumpled. The
cubicle collapsed into a twisted heap of curtain-cloth and metal
rods.

Backing away from the smoldering panel, he whipped out
an automatic, and commanded, "Stick 'em up!"

Quivven obeyed.

"One word, and I'll drill you," said the young man quietly.
"Now walk over here to this door."

Together the two approached the door which opened into
the outside air.

But at just that instant the head of one of the four other men
appeared at the top of the loft stairs. The young man fired, and
the head disappeared.

Then the ant lumbered into sight. Again the man fired. But
it is difficult in the extreme to hit the vital spot of an ant as
large as a horse. Calmly disregarding the shots, the antman
snatched an automatic from the dead body at the top of the
stairs, and fired back.

With a cry of pain, the young man turned away and leaped

into space through the black opening in the side wall of the barn.

Quivven rushed to the stairs.

"Quick, men!" she shouted. "Out and get him. Get him at all costs. There's a twenty-foot drop where he jumped, and he's probably broken his neck."

The sound of a departing car was heard as the men dashed out. Presently they returned to announce sheepishly that a trail of blood led from the barn to where their car had been parked. The car was gone.

"John Blake," mused the antman. "Hm!"

But Quivven was in no mood for musing. Downstairs in the barn there was a telephone. Quickly she called and got a certain Virginia number, and began issuing orders with perfect calmness.

Doggo, the antman, stood by her side, and from time to time nodded his assent or offered suggestions.

MEANWHILE a taxicab, carrying four trussed-up prisoners, arrived at a camp in the Virginia mountains, twenty miles or so west of Washington. The camp was a bustle of activity. Hundreds of men under arms. Other hundreds unarmed, standing in a long waiting-line which led to a brightly lighted laboratory. An administration building, surrounded by parked cars. Inside, pigeons and rats and dogs and some unusually alert-faced human-bodied Whoomangs were receiving final orders.

To this building rushed the taxi driver, and reported, "I've got Kent and Larrabee and two men from the Department of Justice tied up in my cab outside."

"Good!" exclaimed one of the tacticians. "Bring them in. Some one send for Swami Singh. We'll soon find out just how much these fellows know of our plans."

So the four prisoners were dragged in. Sheepishly they stood before the desk. The chief Whoomang swept them with his glance. Then he turned furiously to the taxi driver.

"What does this mean?" he shouted. "None of these men is either Kent or Larrabee!"

Then he regained his self-composure. Rajindra Singh entered the building.

"Swami," exclaimed the chief, "find out who these men are and what they know. Be quick about it."

But at just that moment the telephone rang. It was Quivven, calling from the old barn in Rock Creek Park. The questioning of the prisoners was shelved for the moment, to make way for more important activities.

IT WAS due to Kent's caution that he and Larrabee were not among the captives.

On the way to the office of the Superintendent of Buildings, Kent had faintly caught a glimpse of the back of the head of the taxi driver, and had seen there a telltale scar. When he had gone inside, the first thing that he did was have the superintendent round up all the night attendants of the building. Picking out two who resembled him and Larry in size and age, and slipping each a five-dollar bill to keep them from asking questions, they exchanged clothes.

These two substitutes had been sent in the cab with the two operatives of the Department of Justice.

As soon as the taxi was safely out of sight, Kent and Larrabee and the Assistant Attorney-General had hired another cab, and had set out to inspect all the government barns and storehouses, the least used ones first.

Three or four of these buildings were visited, and developed nothing unusual.

The party were making their way out Sixteenth Street, N.W., just north of the settled part of the city, when they found their way blocked by a large touring car, standing diagonally across the center of the road.

Cautiously Larry got out to investigate, leaving his two companions alertly waiting in the taxicab.

"Now walk over to this door!" he commanded quietly.

"Only one man here," he shouted back, "and he seems to be asleep or drunk."

The others joined him. Together they pulled the body out of the stalled car. It was a young workingman in overalls, and his clothes were wet with sticky blood. They flashed a light in his face.

Then Larry cried out, "It's Jack Blakeslee!"

Jack was still breathing faintly. The taxi driver produced a flask and forced it between the wounded man's teeth. Jack gulped and opened his eyes.

"Hello, Larry," said he, smiling faintly. "Hell of a note! Doggo shot me. But I wrecked their apparatus first. Quivven's there, too, over in Park Commission's old barn. Only four men with them. Hurry, for they'll go to—"

He coughed hoarsely, then tried again. "They'll go to—"

Another paroxysm of coughing, and Jack's body went limp. Kent put his ear to the airman's chest.

"He's dead," he announced sadly.

Laying the body in the car, they started the engine, and ran it to the edge of the road, where they parked it. Jack's automatic and ammunition they gave to the taxi driver. Then they sped on toward the barn which Jack had mentioned as the Whoomang headquarters in his dying breath.

AS THEY neared the barn they heard the roar of a motor and saw the lights of a large plane taking off from the ground. When they reached the barn it was deserted. Inside there was a gasoline motor-generator set still running. There was a wrecked panel and a wrecked matter-transmitting apparatus, such as Kent and Larry had seen before at the camp in the Wisconsin woods. A dead man lay at the top of the stairs. But there was no Quivven, no Doggo, no death-ray machines, and no live Whoomangs.

Crestfallen, they carried the two bodies—Jack's and the dead Whoomang's—back to town, dividing their forces at the parked car which Jack had stolen.

Their expedition had failed.

And they were destined to receive another blow that same night. At the hotel Kent found the following telegram awaiting him:

> They raided the camp in a plane and got Eliot Endicott away.
>
>   VICTOR CHAPIN.

Kent summed up their accomplishments to date:

"We've wrecked two of their matter-transmitting sets and one of their death-ray machines, and have captured two of their camps. The pterodactyl and Cohen are dead. We have plenty of material now to convince the authorities. But, on the other side of the ledger, we don't know where either Helyn or Eliot is. Jack Blakeslee is dead. And Quivven and Doggo are at large and preparing to strike. Oh, if we could only locate them before it is too late!"

"Too bad we didn't have some one follow our two doubles!"

complained Larry. "Then we might have discovered the location of another of their hang-outs."

"Yes, it is," agreed Kent. "Yet, at the time it seemed wiser not to run the risk of making that Whoomang driver suspicious."

He paused for a moment reflectively, then continued, "We have only one day more in which to save America. Yet there's nothing further that we can do to-night. And time so precious, too."

"And meanwhile where is Helyn?" groaned Larry.

CHAPTER XXII

OVER THE TOP

THE LAST THAT they knew of her was when she had been transmitted away from the Wisconsin woods camp of the Whoomangs, just before Aaron Cohen killed himself and the dragon, and Dr. Polakowski wrecked the matter-transmitting set.

An instant later Helyn duly arrived with her two guards at some other headquarters of the organization, she knew not where. Quivven and Doggo were already in the room as she stepped out of the cubicle. An electrician stood at a panel near by.

"Stand by to receive," droned his earphones.

"All ready," he replied.

From within the cubicle there came a thud and a squawk, and the headless body of the great dragon came tumbling and fluttering out, turning somersaults all over the room, very much like a hen fresh from the chopping block. Everybody gasped and scattered. Confusion reigned.

In the midst of this confusion four of Larry's American soldiers, clad in Whoomang overalls, dashed out of the cubicle. Of course they were unarmed, for the metal parts of their rifles and automatics and cartridges had been left behind, up in Wisconsin. But, in the excitement, the enemy forgot this.

One of the Whoomangs screamed, "Here come the Americans!"

The Whoomangs were prepared for even such an emergency.

"Smoke bomb!" commanded Quivven.

Some one threw the bomb, and all the Whoomangs crowded from the room under cover of the ensuing smoke. So also did the four Americans.

When order had been restored Helyn and the four Americans were nowhere to be found.

Search was then made through the entire camp, but it was some time before the Whoomangs ascertained from an unusually dumb guard at one of the gates, that he had let the five fugitives through on some cock-and-bull excuse. He was so rattled by the frantic cross-questioning to which he was subjected, that he couldn't even remember what that excuse had been.

But all around the camp lay the desolate Virginia mountains. Five persons on foot couldn't have traveled very far in this short time. Accordingly human-minded bloodhounds were led to the gate and put on the trail, and soon the beasts were off into the woods in full cry.

Helyn and her four escorts, far off in the mountains, heard the baying and redoubled their speed. They found a mountain road, and followed it upward. Nearer and nearer came the sounds of pursuit.

The road led to a little cabin in a clearing. A peculiar sour alcoholic odor filled the air. On the steps of the cabin sat two bearded men. Two rifles leaned against the door-posts.

As the five fugitives dashed across the clearing, the pack of hounds appeared at its edge.

"Quick!" exclaimed Helyn, with a flash of inspiration. "The revenooers are after us."

Then she sank to the ground exhausted. One of the mountaineers spat reflectively.

"Is thet so?" said he, and reached for his rifle.

"Crack! Crack! Crack! Crack!"

One by one, the bloodhounds—there were four of them—dropped in their tracks.

The man blew down his barrel, and leaned the piece against the door-post once more.

"What be you, ma'am?" he asked. "A lady moonshiner?"

Helyn sat up, panting.

"Yes," she gasped. "And these are four of my bootleg truck-drivers."

"Set down, folks," said the mountaineer to Helyn's four companions. "I reckon no one 'll bother ye up hyar."

Nobody did, for the Whoomangs had no more bloodhounds at this camp.

When the five fugitives had recovered their breath, they concocted a story of a wrecked truck and pursuit by the authorities, which convinced the two simple mountaineers.

By guarded questions, they found out what part of the world they were in, and insisted on getting to Washington at once. But their hosts were sharply insistent that they remain under cover for a while. The mountaineers were so swiftly suspicious of every suggestion of departure that Helyn and her companions were still semi-prisoners in the mountains on the night when Jack Blakeslee had met his heroic death.

BLACKSTONE KENT and Lawrence Larrabee were sitting in their hotel room, disconsolate, when their telephone rang. It was Sir Francis Moxon calling from the hospital. He wanted them to come right up. It was now well after midnight, but they agreed to come. The new operatives, who were guarding their room, had been instructed to let them go wherever they chose, but to accompany them.

So they proceeded to the hospital in two taxicabs, after inspecting heads of both drivers. Kent and Larry rode in separate cabs, each with a Federal operative.

Sir Francis Maxon met them in the reception room.

Swiftly he informed them, "The man who was caught outside

your door, night before last, has been operated on, and has recovered sufficiently to talk. The removal of the moth-grub from his brain has had the same effect on him that it did on your daughter Helyn, namely to restore him to his proper mentality and allegiance, and yet leave unimpaired his memory of all that happened to him while he was a Whoomang. He wants to talk."

"Well, I certainly want him to!" exclaimed Kent.

But when they sought out the house doctor to secure visitors' passes, he demurred.

"That man is too weak, yet," said the physician. "To excite him now, might cause his death."

"I am in charge of this case," snapped Sir Francis, "and that man will talk, if it kills him!"

So the man talked.

First he told about the death-ray machines, and other apparatus, stored in the Rock Creek barn. But his visitors informed him of what had happened at that location.

"Then," said the man, "they will undoubtedly go to their next nearest camp, which is in the mountains just south of Potomac Great Falls."

Blackstone Kent skillfully cross-questioned the man, and became convinced of his absolute sincerity. The man was evidently quite familiar with the Virginia camp. He pointed out its exact location on a map, and described the roads which led to it. Then he dropped back upon his pillows exhausted, and they left him.

Once more alone except for the two detectives in the reception room of the hospital, the three men held a conference of war.

"It's evident that that plane, which rescued Quivven and Doggo, also carried off the death-ray machines," said Larry. "Moreover, we know from this man's story that there are hundreds of fully armed Whoomangs at the Virginia camp. We can't attack it without troops. And how can we persuade the government to give us troops?"

"I have it!" exclaimed Blackstone Kent. "Colonel Burke!"

"And who is Colonel Burke?" asked Larry.

"Joe Burke is a lieutenant-colonel of Marines, stationed at Quantico, about twenty miles south of here," explained Kent. "He is one of nature's noblemen, and an old, old friend of mine. He can't possibly have been made a Whoomang, for the back of his skull is a silver plate, where he was wounded in the battle of Château Thierry. If he had even been kidnaped by the Whoomangs, the matter-transmitting apparatus would have killed him, for his plate would have been left behind. He'll lend me all the troops I need, and will command them in person."

"But will he?" demurred Sir Francis. "It seems to me that no one but a harebrained youth would embark on an adventure such as ours."

"Ah, but you don't know Colonel Joe," Kent retorted. "He loves nothing better than a good scrap. If he's the same old Joe, he'll be tickled to death to turn out the entire Quantico establishment to fight a private war for a friend."

So the three allies, still accompanied by the two detectives, hired two touring cars, and soon were speeding toward Quantico, as fast as the law allowed.

THE SURPRISED sentinel at the gate called the corporal of the guard, and he roused the sergeant of the guard, and he woke up the officer of the guard. The officer of the guard was sufficiently impressed by Kent's distinguished bearing and Sir Francis's monocle, to take a chance and phone the commandant, without first asking permission of the officer of the day.

The commandant was still "the same old Joe." He directed the officer of the guard to send "my distinguished friend, Blackstone Kent" right up, under proper escort. He received his guests at his quarters in pyjamas and Japanese dressing-gown.

He gave full credence to Kent's fantastic tale. Picking up his telephone, he routed the post adjutant out of bed, and gave orders for an inspection of the whole command under full field equipment in twenty minutes. He ordered the supply officer to unlock the ordnance storehouse and be prepared to issue ammunition, and commanded the transportation officer to get out all the trucks. All officers were directed to report to the quarters of the commandant as soon as they were dressed. A squad of men with a corporal were ordered to come right over on the double quick.

"This is something like!" exalted Kent, rubbing his hands.

"You bet your boots it is!" replied the colonel. "I haven't had such fun since the night we tried to blow up the Cattle Show Building in Concord, or the night we swam ashore in Nicaragua. And now, gentlemen, excuse me while I hop upstairs and dress."

The corporal arrived with the squad. Colonel Burke called over the banisters to the corporal to arrest any officer who failed to pass Dr. Moxon's medical examination.

One by one, the officers of the post came smartly in. Sir Francis examined the guard and all passed. He then examined the officers, as they arrived, and ordered the arrest of two of them, without explanation.

A few minutes later, Colonel Burke came down, looking very natty in trench-coat, boots and spurs, campaign hat, and swagger stick. Quickly he checked up on the officers, and ordered the two suspects into solitary confinement, where they were to be allowed to see no one, not even any animals or birds.

At this last remark, they both wilted; but one of them had the courage to demand belligerently, "I have a right to know the charges against me, sir."

"Yes, you have," admitted the colonel, readily enough. "I'll furnish you a copy in the morning. The headquarters stenographer doesn't happen to be up at this time of night."

So that was that.

Then the companies were inspected. No more scars. Good!

"March your companies to the storehouse, for the issue of full war ammunition. Then to the trucks," he commanded.

A few minutes later the entire military personnel of the Quantico Marine Base, with the exception of the officer of the day, the officer of the guard, the guard, the two prisoners, and the air forces, were on the road in trucks and automobiles, bound northwesterly into the Virginia mountains. Quantico is located on the Potomac River, about twenty miles due south of Washington, D.C. The enemy camp was about twenty miles a little north of west from Washington, and thus was about thirty-five miles northwest of Quantico.

Blackstone Kent and Colonel Burke rode in the latter's car at the head of the column. As they rumbled along, they studied a map with the aid of a flash light.

"**MY PLAN** of campaign is as follows," announced Colonel Burke. "Instead of driving right down this road"—pointing to one on the map—"which runs to their camp, I shall take this other road, which will bring us about four miles to the south of them. There are mountains in between—see—and the contours are pretty close together, which means steep mountains, but there are ravines indicated here, and it should be possible to scramble up one of those ravines somehow. Thus we can take the enemy by surprise."

Having laid out this general plan, the colonel passed the map to his adjutant—who was sitting in front with the driver—and instructed that officer where to go, and where to unload.

Then he questioned Kent in detail about the probable numbers, disposition and armament of the enemy. Larry, Sir Francis, and the two operatives rode in other cars.

Along toward morning they reached their destination, formed, and started up a gully into the mountains. The gully finally petered out on a plateau, across which they marched due north. Soon thereafter they encountered thick woods and thicker shrubbery.

The sky was overcast, and presently, in spite of their compasses, the officers were all mixed up. Maps were produced, but the officers were unable to identify their position.

Morning began to dawn, cold and gray, and all around them was nothing but rocks and woods and wilderness.

Then some one announced that he had sighted a house. At once a number of officers went forward and knocked on the door. It was opened by a black-bearded old man, who promptly held both hands aloft above his head.

"Where's yer search warrant?" he demanded. "I know my rights."

"No, no, old-timer," expostulated one of the officers. "Put down your hands. We're not after you. We're merely lost."

A second mountaineer, with a rifle held alertly in both hands, appeared behind the first. And then a girl, and four young men in overalls.

"Helyn!" exclaimed a voice out of the dusk from behind the officers.

"Larry!" she cried, recognizing his voice.

And soon the two were in each other's arms.

With this introduction, friendly relations were soon established. Kent came forward and embraced his long-lost child. She had learned from her four companions that he was still alive and had led the Wisconsin revolt. Kent warmly shook hands with his four lost Wisconsin recruits. There were introductions all around.

Then Colonel Burke explained to the two mountaineers that this expedition was for the purpose of forestalling an expected attempt to assassinate the President. Helyn and her four alleged truckmen now admitted to their hosts that they had been fleeing from the assassins, rather than from "revenooers."

"Well, durned!" exclaimed one of the mountaineers. "Brother and me was in the Spanish War. We can't let anything like thet go on right in our own front yard, ye mout say. Cain't we enlist?"

"Swear 'em in, judge," said the colonel to Blackstone Kent, wishing to make it impressive.

So Kent had them raise their right hands aloft, and asked them, "Do you solemnly swear to support the Constitution of the United States, and defend it against all its enemies?"

"Yes, sir, I do," they replied, but one of them added, "Leastwise excepting the Eighteenth Amendment."

Kent let it go at that.

THE TWO mountaineers then got their squirrel-rifles, put on their boots, and led off into the woods. Helyn was left behind, with a squad of Marines to guard her. By now it was almost daylight.

Finally their guides halted them.

"Jest over thet rise ahead, is the camp," they announced.

Colonel Burke asked them some questions, and then deployed his forces. One platoon, he sent with the two guides, to circle the enemy's left flank and strike at the powerhouse, explaining to them the absolute necessity of putting the dynamos out of commission before the death-rays could be turned on the main body.

"When you reach the powerhouse, your lieutenant will fire two shots in quick succession with his forty-five; then wait an instant, and fire one more. That will be our signal to attack."

He dispatched the platoon, then called in his officers, to give them their final battle orders.

After a considerable wait, the signal sounded, *"Crack, crack— crack!"*

With a cheer, the Marines went over the top.

The camp was taken completely by surprise, and it was well that it was, for the attackers were greatly outnumbered. The Whoomangs soon rallied, and their heavy fire forced the Marines to take temporary cover.

An advance picket crept back and reported to Colonel Burke, "Sir, they are wheeling out some funny-looking searchlights behind that building just opposite our center, and are pointing them our way, right through the building."

The colonel looked anxiously at a few electric lights which were still burning in the camp, in spite of the rising sun.

If those lights didn't go out pretty soon, it would mean that the flank attack on the powerhouse had failed. And then would come the searing death-ray.

CHAPTER XXIII

WAR TO THE DEATH

THE PLATOON, GUIDED by the two mountaineers, crept to the powerhouse, the door of which was open. The hum of the generators mingled with the *putt-putt-putt* of the gasoline engine which drove them.

The lieutenant in command fired the three signal shots and gave the order to attack.

But, even as they reached the door, some one slammed it shut. A heavy steel affair it was, bolted securely to the brick walls of the little building. Quickly the soldiers circled the building, but steel shutters were promptly closed on all the windows. Quite evidently the Whoomangs were prepared for just such an emergency.

The lieutenant directed his men to form a pyramid at the first telephone pole. But scarcely had the men got halfway up, when they crumpled to the ground. The pole had been electrified. The Whoomangs were prepared for this, too.

The lieutenant was frantic.

"If we don't cut off the current within the next few minutes," he exclaimed, "our entire force is doomed."

"Would cuttin' them wires do?" inquired one of the mountaineers, pointing aloft.

"Certainly," snapped the lieutenant a bit testily, "but who's going to do it?"

"I aim tew," drawled the Virginian. Then raising his squirrel rifle, he let fly several times. At each shot one of the wires parted.

Soon the powerhouse was completely severed from the rest of the camp.

Fortunately the men who had suffered the electric shock were not badly hurt, merely stunned. The lieutenant formed his platoon, deployed it, and attacked the enemy in the flank. And with them stalked the two black-bearded men, firing steadily, and making every shot tell.

Meanwhile Colonel Burke, anxiously watching the lights of the camp, saw them suddenly flicker out. Of course, this might mean the demolition of the powerhouse, or it might merely mean that some one had noticed the arrival of morning.

If the first explanation were correct, it was safe to attack, and the enemy morale would be sadly shattered by the failure of their greatest weapon. And even if the second explanation were correct, he might just as well attack, for his forces would shortly be annihilated anyway. So he gave the order to charge.

The Whoomangs were caught between the cross-fire of Burke's forces and the platoon which had been sent to attack the powerhouse. They had depended on the death-ray machines, and those diabolical implements had failed them. After a brief stand they ran.

But even as they did so, an airplane rose from the midst of their camp and soared away, amid a vain fusillade of shots from the victors.

And then a flight of pigeons rose from the administration building.

"Shoot those birds!" shouted Kent excitedly.

"Yer really want 'em?" asked one of the mountaineers dubiously.

"For God's sake, yes!" exclaimed Kent.

"Come on, brother," remarked the other casually, and raising their rifles, they brought down every bird.

Colonel Burke took over the camp. Once more in the history of the Marine Corps, the Marines had arrived and had the situation well in hand. Every animal which the victors found was promptly slaughtered, despite the human expression in their eyes.

The beleaguered powerhouse surrendered. Every building was searched.

The four men who had been captured in the taxicab were found and released. The Whoomangs were herded into barracks and placed under guard. Not even the doctors and nurses were spared, for the conventions of war did not apply to such a conflict as this. Patrols were dispatched into the surrounding woods to round up stragglers.

BUT IT soon became evident that Quivven and Doggo had escaped again. Another Pyrrhic victory for Kent! And "The Day" was to be to-morrow! Kent had only that day and night in which to forestall the *coup d'état*.

Well, at least he had the satisfaction of realizing that he was being somewhat annoying to the enemy. He had broken up three of their establishments, he and Larry were still alive and free, and his daughter Helyn was safe once more.

Breakfast was found half completed, was taken over by Marine Corps K.P.s, and was served to the victors in the Whoomang mess-hall.

It was then decided that Kent and Larry and Sir Francis and the detectives should return at once to Washington, and Colonel Burke to Quantico. Helyn would be safer in the mountain cabin of the moonshiners, until "The Day" had come and gone. Much as Larry longed to be with her, he realized where his duty lay.

So they helped themselves to several of the fine cars parked around the administration building, and set out, leaving one of Burke's majors in command of the captured camp.

Before they reached the point where the roads to Washington and Quantico forked, a Marine private on a motorcycle met them, and held up his hand for them to stop. To Colonel Burke he handed a dispatch.

The colonel read it, and then his face suffused with smiles. He strode over to Kent's car.

"Listen to this. The officer of the day at Quantico reports that one of our aviators has just phoned in that he attacked and brought down an enemy plane, and has captured a big black bug and a furry lady all covered with fur—can you feature that?—'a furry lady all covered with fur.' That's just what it says here, a furry—"

"Yes, yes, go on!" interrupted Kent.

"And one wounded man and one dead man," continued Burke lamely. "Well, anyhow, this dispatch gives us the map position. Come on, let's go there."

He mentioned two numbers on the artillery grid system which were absolutely unintelligible to his civilian auditors, but which apparently constituted quite explicit directions to the Marine privates who were driving the cars; and soon they were all dashing down another road.

It was not long before they pulled up at a field in which lay three airplanes, two of which were neatly parked, and the third rather badly smashed up. The huge black antman and Quivven the Goldenflame stood facing two Marine enlisted men and one Marine officer. Beside them on the ground lay two motionless human forms, one of which was tenderly wrapped in blankets. Another Marine officer advanced and saluted as Colonel Burke and his friends approached.

"Sir," reported the young flyer, "we took off at daybreak, just as you ordered, and flew toward the spot where you told us the enemy camp was located. We heard the sounds of fighting, and then saw a plane come up, so we tried to head it off. It cut loose at us with a machine gun, sir, so we fired back, and it crashed. The driver's done for, sir; we shot him up pretty badly. But the bug and the yellow lady don't seem hurt at all. The other fellow seems to have been wounded before. He was wrapped up in blankets when we found him."

As they approached the group, Quivven's lip curled with scorn.

"So it's you, Sergeant Stone?" said she. "The traitor who led the new men against his own Whoomangs up at the Wisconsin camp?"

"No, madam," replied Kent, with a smile. "It's Blackstone Kent, whose nephew and daughter you kidnaped, who was drowned at sea, and who has been on your trail all summer."

"Your nephew is over there," announced Quivven, dramatically indicating the still figure swathed in blankets.

Kent and Sir Francis hastened to Eliot's side.

"He's in a bad way," reported the doctor, after a hurried examination. "We must get him to a hospital at once."

"We have a fine hospital at Quantico," suggested Colonel Burke.

"Then let's get him there right away," asserted Kent, "and the golden lady, too."

So Eliot Endicott was carried, and Quivven the Goldenflame was led to the waiting cars.

"LET'S BUMP off the big ant," suggested the colonel. "He's only an insect."

"No, no!" Kent demurred. "We may need him yet."

"Thank you," replied Quivven sweetly. "We have influential friends in Washington. Before tomorrow night the President will be ordering our release."

"I rather think not," asserted Kent grimly.

"You do, do you?" countered Quivven. "Well, I might just as well be frank with you. Your capturing Doggo and me won't in the least interfere with the plans of our organization. So treat us carefully, if you value your lives. We can be grateful, if you act so as to deserve gratitude."

"Her confidence rather gives one a chill," remarked Larry aside to Sir Francis Moxon.

So Eliot Endicott and Quivven were rushed to Quantico. The huge ant was left in the field, under guard, until an army truck could be sent after him.

Larry also went to Quantico, but Kent hurried to Washington to report to the Attorney-General. That official refused to believe the latest news until he had phoned to the Marine base and had talked personally to the commandant.

Then he warmly shook Kent's hand and said, "Tell me anything whatever from now on, and I'll believe you. But what are we to do now? Undoubtedly all the enemy plans have already been made for to-morrow, and will not need the guiding hands of those two creatures."

"We must examine the heads of all the Cabinet," asserted Kent, and arrest the two Whoomang members."

But the Attorney-General refused. Even with the downfall of the government staring him in the face, he could not bring himself to risk offending the rest of the Cabinet.

"It can't be the Secretary of the Navy," he began, "for if it were, Colonel Burke would have been reprimanded by now. It can't be—"

Kent interrupted. "If you won't take the obvious course, there's no use to sit around and guess who's who. Put extra guards on the President and Cabinet, then, and let it go at that. I've done all that I can. I've been practically without sleep for several days and nights. I'm not as young as I used to be, and so I'm going back to my hotel and turn in. Let me have an extra guard, too, if you please."

"You aren't going to give up and desert us, are you?" exclaimed the Attorney-General. "Can't you at least suggest something for us to do?"

"I made my suggestion, and you rejected it," replied Kent coldly.

"But suggest something else."

"All right," said Kent. "Notify the District police that you must locate two important criminals today or to-night, a man and a woman, and that their only identifying feature is that each of them has a scar at the base of the skull. You might even tell the Police Commissioner that unless the man and the woman are arrested before daybreak to-morrow, the President's life will be in grave danger.

"Tell the Commissioner that the man may even be a member of the force, so that he must first look over the entire force for scars. Use whatever influence or cajolery you can, and get him to put every patrolman, traffic cop, and detective to work to run these two alleged individuals down for you, and to arrest as a suspicious character every person having such a scar. This ought to result in rounding up a considerable number of the enemy, and may so hamper their plans, by removing a few key individuals, that they will be forced to postpone 'The Day,' and give us a chance to combat them."

"A good idea!" exclaimed the Attorney-General. "I hate inaction."

"Then stir up enough action for the two of us. I've got to rest," asserted Kent. "Remember the extra guard, please. And phone me, if anything interesting develops."

Then, although it was only just about noon, Blackstone Kent went to bed and was soon fast asleep.

THE POLICE dragnet rounded up quite a few persons with scars, but it was not possible to ascertain whether they were Whoomangs, or if so, just how important they were to the plans for the morrow.

About midnight Kent was awakened by the insistent ringing of his telephone. The call purported to be from Sir Francis Moxon at the Marine hospital, urging Kent to come immediately to Quantico. Sir Francis wouldn't tell him what for. So Kent agreed, and started to dress.

Then it occurred to him that this might be a trap, so he called the Marine Base and asked for the commandant, by whom he verified the call.

So Kent hired three touring cars, examined the drivers for scars, and started for Quantico, taking two detectives with him in one car, and preceded and followed by cars each containing one detective. As the fatal Day drew near he was becoming more and more cautious.

As he left the hotel he glanced at his watch. Just 12.01 A.M. The fatal Day had arrived.

He reached Quantico about one in the morning. The sentry at the gate was expecting him, and let him right in. Soon he was in conference with Larry and Colonel Burke and Sir Francis. The object of sending for him was this Quivven had rallied from her operation with unexpected rapidity, but refused to talk.

So Blackstone Kent went to see her. Gone were all her ambitions and dreams of empire, for she was no longer a Whoomang. And yet she refused to give them any assistance in preventing the carrying out of the Whoomang plans.

"What's it to me?" she persisted dully. "I am not of your Earth. Your affairs do not concern me. I am a Vairking of the planet Venus. Let me go back to my own planet and rest after this terrible experience."

In vain Kent argued and threatened and cajoled. Here was the key to the whole situation, but the key refused to turn in the lock.

And then Kent thought of the golden princess's love for Eliot Endicott. He withdrew and conferred with Sir Francis. Eliot was reported as being very low, but conscious. Kent conferred with his nephew, and then had the young man's bed wheeled in beside that of Quivven.

For a few moments the two of then gazed hungrily at each other, and then Eliot held out his hand feebly, and Quivven took it. Her eyes were wet with tears; she was visibly affected.

"Is it true, Quivven dearest," he asked, "that you are no longer a Whoomang, and that you are no longer determined to rule the world?"

"It is true, Eliot," said she.

"And you still love me?"

"I do, forever."

"Quivven, Goldenflame," said he, "I followed you, and you alone. I fought for you personally, not for the Whoomang cause. It was for you that I betrayed my country. And now that you no longer care one way or the other, won't you help these men to save America?"

"You love your country?"

"Second only to you, Quivven."

"And it would give you pleasure for me to save your country?"

"It would go a long way toward enabling me to hold up my head again, and face the world, Quivven."

"For you, Eliot, I will do it." Then, turning to Kent, she asked, "Well, what is it that you wish me to do for you?"

Eliot Endicott slumped back, exhausted. He had partially atoned for his faithlessness to his official oath.

Quickly Kent and Quivven discussed details. An extension telephone was strung in to the bed of the Princess. And then she called a certain Washington number.

"**HELLO!**... Fairfield?... Oh, this is you, is it? This is her majesty speaking. Get me Fairfield at once.... Yes, it's important. Am I accustomed to give orders which are not important?... It will take between a half or three-quarters of an hour, you say? Very well, then, have Fairfield call me at Alexandria 168, just as soon as you can get hold of him.... Good-by."

"But—but—" Colonel Burke sputtered, "Alexandria 168 isn't our number."

"Isn't it?" replied Quivven archly. "Then it had better become so, quite quickly, if you would save your beloved America. Wouldn't I have been a fool if I had given my man the correct number of the Marine Base? He has brains enough to make inquiries before he calls back."

"I take off my hat to your majesty," said Kent; then, snatching up the phone, "Alexandria chief operator, please.... Hello! Chief operator? This is Operative Kent of the Department of Justice, calling from Quantico Marine Base.... You'll have to take my word for it; I can't show you my badge over the phone very well, can I?... Tell me, have you a number 168?... Good! If any one calls that number in the next hour, connect them with the Marine Base, without explanation."

A long pause while the telephone official replied, then Kent hung up the receiver and said in a disgusted tone, "He refuses to do it. Come on, Burke, you've got to drive me, like the devil, over to Alexandria, and identify me to that pup!"

So they left Quivven and Eliot lying hand in hand, and hastened out into the night. It was now about two o'clock in the morning of the Day set for the great Whoomang revolution.

Before leaving the Marine Base they had the *Post* operator plug line No. 4 permanently to Quivven's phone.

At Alexandria they experienced but little difficulty in persuading the telephone company official that they were genuine—luckily, being sufficiently impressed with the colonel's uniform, he didn't ask to see Kent's non-existent badge.

The official agreed to put through, to the fourth line of the Marine Base, any call for 168, and to tell any inquirer that that number represented a lonely house in the suburbs of the city. Kent was permitted to examine the heads of all the operators, on the pretense that he was looking for an escaped female prisoner with a peculiar birthmark under her hair.

Just as Kent and Burke were about to leave, one of the girls smiled and nodded to the chief operator.

"Here's your party now," said he. "Would you like to listen in?"

They eagerly assented, and were furnished earphones, and were plugged into the line. They heard Fairfield, whoever he was, call Quivven, and guardedly identify himself and her.

Then she asked, "You learned of the capture of our camp at Potomac Great Falls, and of my subsequent escape?"

Yes, he had learned that she and Doggo had made a safe get-away in a plane. The organization had been waiting for word of the two of them ever since.

"Well," said Quivven, "we are safe and in hiding on the out-skirts of Alexandria. Important changes will have to be made in to-day's plans."

"I hope they are not to be called off!" murmured Fairfield.

"Your enthusiasm does you credit," replied the Princess. "Not called off, but merely materially altered in order to make the result more certain, in view of recent events. So I want you to get in touch with every man, woman, and animal who has a part assigned in to-day's great events. Tell them all to gather at Station G, just before sunrise. Tell them to leave their autos at quite a distance, and walk, so as to attract no attention.

"No lights at the station. Keep well under cover within the building, and expect me by airplane just at sunrise. And now go away from your phone, but leave one man there who can get in touch with you. I shall leave this phone; for we may have been overheard, and detectives may even now be hastening to the houses of our two numbers."

"Every detail shall be carried out to the letter, your majesty."

Quivven and her minion both hung up.

BLACKSTONE KENT pointed out to Colonel Burke, "Now, all that we have to do is to find Station G, and surround it. We'll need troops for that."

So the colonel called the recently captured camp near Great Falls, and ordered the major, whom he had left in charge, to entrain at once for Washington, with all the men he could spare, and to expect further orders *en route*.

Then thanking the chief operator, they hurried back to Quantico, reaching there about half past three in the morning.

Quivven the Goldenflame was asleep, her hand still clasping that of Eliot Endicott. Quickly they roused her, and inquired the location of Station G. It turned out to be the same, Rock Creek barn where Jack Blakeslee had demolished the matter-transmitting apparatus, and had received his death wound.

Then Quivven said, "Eliot, dear, your hand is cold from

holding it out to my bed like this. Better tuck it in for a little while."

She released it, and it slumped to the floor.

"He's dead!" she shrieked.

Sir Francis Moxon came running. Sure enough, Eliot Endicott was dead. He had made his final atonement.

"Oh, you Americans!" screamed Quivven. "You killed my Eliot! Your bullets did it! Oh, how I hate you! But I'll undo what I have just done to help you! It is not yet too late."

And she seized the telephone.

But Kent and the colonel wrenched it from her hands.

Meanwhile Sir Francis had been quickly rummaging in his medicine-case. Striding over to Quivven's bed, he suddenly jabbed a hypodermic needle into her side.

"Tell them to keep away from Station G!" she shouted. "Let the Great Day be carried out exactly as planned."

She sank back on the pillows and turned triumphant though fast-dulling eyes at the men who surrounded her. "I am sleepy," said she. "I have been drugged. But I got my message off in time. Even now it is on its way to Fairfield. My Eliot will be avenged."

Meanwhile a large gray cat sneaked out from under Quivven's bed and slunk down the aisle between the cots of the hospital.

But Kent went always armed, these days. Drawing his revolver, he brought down the sneaking Whoomang messenger cat. His ability as a pistol shot, which had won him his sergeantcy among the Whoomangs, once more stood him in good stead.

He could not tell, however, whether any other Whoomang animals had heard the last frantic words of the drugged golden princess and were already on the way with the message.

HAD QUIVVEN planned to double cross them, anyway? It looked like it now, for how else could one explain the presence of the cat under her bed, and known to her? Its presence must have been known to her, or she would not have been so confident of the delivery of her message. But they could only speculate on this, for the cat was dead; and Quivven was by now in a deeply drugged slumber.

Another cat stuck its head in the door of the hospital ward. Quickly Kent drew, and fired again. But, as he did so, Colonel Burke knocked up his hand. The bullet went wide, and the cat stealthily vanished.

Kent turned furiously upon his friend.

"Damn it, man," he rasped, "why did you do that?"

"You have animals on the brain," replied Burke soothingly. "That was our regimental mascot. We can't have you killing her, you know."

"Prove it!" snapped Kent.

So Burke went and got Tabby and brought her in. She had no scars. Kent sheepishly joined in the general mirth.

Then the colonel wrote out orders, which he sent by motorcycle to the Marine troops who were on their way to Washington. Also he instructed his two planes to set out for the Rock Creek barn just before sunrise.

Meanwhile Kent got the Attorney-General on the phone—that official was anxiously spending the night at the Department of Justice—and asked him to locate the house of the telephone number which Quivven had called, arrest the scarred man whom he would find there, and try and ascertain from him the whereabouts of a man named Fairfield.

Kent was fearful lest Quivven's recall message might have got out, or that Quivven might have lied to them as to the location of Station G, and he meant to do everything possible to forestall the enemy.

Then he went to take a look at the warehouse where they had Doggo chained and guarded. The huge antman was still there, all right, and the lawyer could not resist the temptation of taunting him.

"The great Day has come, Doggo," said he.

" 'But not yet gone, Cæsar,'" the antman quoted back at him. "You see, I know some of the literature of you humans."

This gave Kent an idea. Doggo must be removed as a menace. There must be no Whoomang ant for the new President to release, if the coup should still succeed. So Kent sought out Sir Francis.

"But I'm no veterinary," objected the doctor.

"Nevertheless, it must be done," asserted Kent; so the doctor agreed.

CHAPTER XXIV

MOPPING UP

LEAVING LARRY TO watch the sleeping Quivven, Kent and Burke, with half the operatives, motored as rapidly as possible to Washington. The colonel, to take charge of his troops; and the lawyer, to inform the Attorney-General of developments.

That official at once requisitioned the riot squad of the city police and had it held in readiness under the Sixteenth Street viaduct. Then he sent several of his best operatives to spy on the supposedly vacant barn. These made contact with the advance pickets of the main body of the Marines, which was deployed in the bed of Rock Creek in the vicinity of the swimming hole.

All reported that no men had been observed approaching the old barn. It was now nearly dawn of the great Day. The sun rose over the eastern Maryland hills. The old barn stood out bleak and bare on the hillside. From the southward came the drone of an airplane. A motorcycle cop, driving slowly down Sixteenth Street from the north, stopped at a point from which the building was not concealed by the trees. From the valley of Rock Creek a long skirmish-line of Marines crept stealthily upward toward the old barn.

The airplane landed in a vacant field beside the barn and taxied up almost to the door. Still no signs of life. One of the aviators got out and approached the door with drawn revolver, while the other aimed the machine gun of the craft squarely at the building.

The man who was on foot flung open the door, then stepped back a pace. Within the barn the early morning sun disclosed a throng of men, women, and animals. They had all arrived there long before the Marine scouts and the Department of Justice detectives; for Quivven had urged them, through Fairfield, to keep under cover, and they had been most successful in so doing. For a moment they stood surprised, irresolute. Then some one within fired a shot at the aviator, and several made a rush for the door.

But just at that instant the machine gun cut loose, not at the throng inside but around it, as a warning, and the Whoomang hordes slunk back into the darkness of the interior.

The waiting motorcycle cop on Sixteenth Street sped full speed to the southward, with his siren going full blast.

Out from one the cellar doors of the barn, on the side away from the aviators, poured the Whoomang forces, only to be driven back again by the charging Marines.

Then, with the roar of many motors, there arrived the riot squad of the District police. The Marines surrounded the building, and let the riot squad go in and do the mopping up. There was surprisingly little resistance inside, for the spirit of the enemy was broken without their leaders.

A few pigeons rose from the cupola of the barn, but the second Marine aircraft, just then arriving, circled after them and shot them down, one by one, with machine gun fire. The victory was complete.

Blackstone Kent, and the Attorney-General, and Colonel Burke solemnly shook hands, as the sun rose and shone full upon the nation they had saved.

Then the police sergeant in charge called for the patrol wagons, and Kent phoned the glad news to Sir Francis Moxon and Lawrence Larrabee, anxiously awaiting at Quantico.

"You're in charge, Sir Francis!" shouted Larry, and seizing

the first car he could lay his hands on, sped off to the mountain cabin and Helyn.

THERE is not much more to tell. Of course, the President was informed of the whole story. The two Whoomang members of the Cabinet were identified, were quietly seized by Secret Service men, and were restored to normal by the surgical skill of Sir Francis Moxon, to their deep gratitude.

Blackstone Kent brought his legal ability into play by organizing a chain of corporations to take over all the property which had been amassed by the criminal organization. These corporations were administered by him for the benefit of the ex-Whoomangs, who had formerly been employed on the various undertakings of the triumvirate.

Deprived of their leaders, most of the Whoomangs appeared to become stricken with a sort of numbing fear, and hence merely waited dumbly in their various camps for the arrival of Kent and his conquering forces, who had Sir Francis Moxon and Dr. Victor Chapin superintend the work of restoring them to a human state.

Many of the more brainy of the Whoomangs resisted, but against them Kent always employed the following tactics, with almost invariable success. The objector would be seized, legally or otherwise, and would be promptly operated on. The operation would restore him to normal, and that would be the end of his armed or legal opposition.

Among the electrical experts of the Whoomang organization were found men capable of recreating the superpowerful matter-transmitting set, with which the gray dragon and the huge antman and the golden Princess had been brought down from the Planet Venus by Aaron Cohen. Neither of the survivors of this triumvirate cared to remain on earth, nor did they, restored to normal, wish to be sent back to the land of the Whoomangs on Venus.

So Kent's electrical experts finally got in touch with Myles Standish Cabot, the Radio Man, formerly of Boston, but now regent of the Kingdom of Cupia on Venus. At Quivven's request, nothing was said about her, but Cabot was notified that his old friend Doggo wished to come back to him.

When all was ready, Quivven, too, stepped within the coordinate axes, the proper formula was repeated, the switches were closed, and Doggo the Formian and Quivven the Goldenflame passed from the ken of mankind.

Lawrence Larrabee married Helyn Kent in Washington, D.C., at a wedding which was one of the leading events of the social season, and which was attended by the President and Cabinet, the British ambassador, and the entire Marine establishment from Quantico. He is fast becoming Kent's right-hand man.

Dr. Victor Chapin married pretty little blue-eyed Alice, who insisted on it as soon as her operation made her human once more. And on a visit to Larry, he confided, with a touch of retrospective sadness in his voice, "You know, Alice was much more docile when she was a Whoomang."

ABOUT THE AUTHOR

THE IDENTITY OF Ralph Milne Farley is shrouded in mystery. When his first story, "The Radio Man," appeared in the *Argosy—All-Story Weekly*, in 1924, it was announced editorially that the author was the world's leading authority in two lines, to name either of which would be instantly to reveal his identity.

"The Radio Man" attracted considerable attention and comment in literary and technical circles, and one newspaper, the Boston *Post*, even put one of its best sleuth-hounds on the trail. By careful study of the internal evidence in the story, especially the fact that the narrative started on Chappaquiddick Island, off the coast of Massachusetts, and that the hero was described as a member of the Harvard class of 1909, the *Post* narrowed the field to two Harvard '09 men who own estates on the island in question: namely, Dr. Francis M. Rackermann and former State Senator Roger Sherman Hoar. Dr. Rackemann is a recognized authority on hay-fever and eczema; whereas Senator Hoar has written the outstanding American texts on "Constitutional Conventions" and on "Ballistics."

Recently apropos Farley's "The Radio Flyers," the Boston *Post* announced that further evidence, namely a similarity between certain passages in one of Farley's stories and a whimsy entitled "Blue Dandelions," published years ago by Senator Hoar in the *Atlantic Monthly*, definitely establishes their identity. The *Post* ought to know, as Hoar used to work for them.

So we are accepting this verdict, and are publishing the portrait of the Senator.

Hon. Roger Sherman Hoar (alias Ralph Milne Farley), was born in Waltham, Massachusetts, on April 8, 1887. Until eight years ago he lived in Concord, Massachusetts.

He holds three degrees from Harvard University. In addition to his service in the State Senate, he has been Assistant Attorney General of Massachusetts, and Legal Advisor of the Constitution-

Ralph Milne Farley

al Convention of 1917. He resigned that position to enlist as a private at the outbreak of the World War. Rapidly rising to captain, he served as senior instructor in military surveying at the Coast Artillery School, and later on the Technical Staff.

After the war, Bucyrus Company, of South Milwaukee, Wisconsin, the largest manufacturer of excavating machinery in America, was looking for a combined lawyer and engineer to take charge of their legal affairs, and persuaded Captain Hoar to resign his commission. He is now the attorney of their successor, Bucyrus-Erie Company. On the side, he is Lecturer in Physics at Marquette University, and a reserve major of the Technical Staff of the United States Army.

Major Hoar is the author of a number of works on law and engineering, and is a contributor to legal and technical magazines.

He is the inventor of several patented devices," including the north-finding apparatus used by his hero, *Eric Redmond,* in "The Radio Flyers." This is an actual practical instrument, useful in aiming big guns, the patent to which is owned by the War Department.

His chief interests, outside his official position, are his family, higher mathematics, blue dandelions and writing.

He is married, has a daughter and two sons, and lives in South Milwaukee.

Although each of his titles contains the word "Radio," he has never owned a radio set. No item of the technical background of any of his stories has ever been successfully challenged.

THE ARGOSY LIBRARY™

THE BEST FICTION
FROM THE FRANK
A. MUNSEY LINE